A ЯEVERSE HAREM STORY

KER DUKEY

K WEBSTER

Cover Design: Amy Queau
Photo: Adobe Stock
Editor: Emily A. Lawrence, Lawrence Editing
Formatting: Champagne Book Design

For those of you who are a sucker for the romantic stuff…

like butt sex and ass spanking.

PROLOGUE

Clove Sterling—The Client

Seventeen Years Old…

Heavy, wet tears drop to my cheeks, causing me to sniffle to contain the sorrow pouring out of me.

My heart feels too heavy, cracking inside my chest like a glass paperweight being dropped into the rocks of the ocean. People around me watch me with sympathy and pity. I hate it. They don't know me—no one does. Mom was the only person who really knew me, truly, and now she's gone. I'm really alone.

Dad's hand grips mine tight as if to remind me that's not true…only it is. He mumbles down at me to wipe my tears, stuffing a tissue in my face with his free hand. He loves me, but he loves his career more, and I've always known my place in the world he created for himself. Mom knew her place too, and she performed her role like she was created to be a politician's wife. Grown in a field and picked as the ripest wife. Perfect childbearing hips, pretty face, refined grooming, well-taught manners and views on world topics, but not too much to be confused with her thinking her opinions matter.

She was there as a prop to my dad, and I was an extension of that prop. Americans loved nothing more than a family man with home values.

When the crowd finally parts, Dad begins to tug me away from the hole in the ground they lowered my mother's casket into. The urge to pull free and throw myself down there with her is so strong, Dad has to tighten his hold on me like I'm a petulant child. His eyes scorn me, frown lines tugging down his brow. Will I ever be allowed to grow up?

Set myself free, give myself some room to just breathe and accept I'm alone.

Swallowing my grief, I dig deep for courage and allow Dad to drag me away.

His crisp blue suit stands out in contrast against everyone else wearing black. Mom always loved him in blue. She bought him that suit. A rock has formed in my throat, restricting me from speaking when a woman joins us and asks me a question no one should have to answer minutes after burying her mother.

"How are you coping with the passing of your mother?"

"Not now," my father barks toward her. Flashes of camera lights spark in my face, stunning me and causing me to almost stumble backward in the silly heels my dad's PR team insisted I wore. Who knew I needed to be dressed a certain way to appeal to the public at my own mother's funeral. But Marjorie—Dad's own personal public relations advisor—insists I must sparkle, even in his shadow.

Before I actually fall to the ground, a pair of strong arms come around my waist to steady me, making a little gasp whisper through my parted lips. Before I have time to gain back my equilibrium a wall of muscle surrounds us. Four men shielding us from the glare of the lens. Their backs protecting me from the overzealous media trying to impose on such a delicate time in my life.

I'm ushered by the man behind me toward a black limo parked on the grass verge. His arm grips me against his firm, built body, his jacket coming around me to hide my face as the other three men in front of us move until we reach the car and I'm deposited inside. My chest is tight and my breathing is ragged from the ordeal. Before I have time to compose myself, all four men accompany me within the car, causing a trickle of fear to engulf me when one sidles up next to me. Scanning them one by one, no recognition sparks and I'm about to flee when the door reopens and my dad gets in with us. Exhaling the breath I'd been holding, I fidget a little in my seat, knowing all eyes are trained on me.

My gaze travels around the array of bodies, all eyes piercing and penetrating something inside of me I can't grasp a hold of or explain. Strong jaws, defined features, and muscles that strain their suits. They look like something from an action movie.

"Clove, this is my new security team. Integral Defense Security. They'll be looking after us from now on," my dad announces before typing something into his cell phone.

Taking them all in, my mouth opens and closes, causing the one sitting in front of us to smirk.

"Clove, huh? Like a four-leaf clover?" He smiles, his hazel eyes curious and slightly amused. I frown in response. "Ford Cross," he says before pulling open his jacket to reveal a gun and three knives carefully tucked away. "Executive Weapons Specialist. Pleased to meet you."

"Nice to meet you too," I mutter, leaning back in my seat some.

"It's okay," the one next to me informs me, his shoulder nudging into mine like we're old friends. His cologne surrounds me, filling the air with an intoxicating scent of citrus and coconut water. My eyes lift to meet his. Bright green, enchanting eyes. Golden skin to match his golden-brown hair. He practically glows, like a handsome prince from one of my fantasy novels. "The name's Leo. Leo King. I'm IDS's Open Source Intelligence Agent. In a nutshell, I find out anything and everything about everyone. You're safe now and we will always be here to protect you from them," he says, nodding toward the throngs of people outside the limo, "and anyone else."

Both men seem genuine, kind, and fierce. My nerves settle a bit until someone bangs on the window. Ford already has his hand inside his jacket and out with his gun drawn before I can even turn my head toward the sound.

"Jack," Marjorie hollers, tapping the glass again. "They aren't going to let you leave without some sort of statement."

Dad pats my knee and kisses my cheek before giving Marjorie a nod that has her stepping away from the door. "Take her back to the house for the wake. I'm going to deal with the press," my dad notifies the men and then opens the car door. He leaves me inside with these four strangers who just concealed my sorrow from the world to view.

"Lucky little Clove," Ford says with a smirk as he tucks his gun away, "you can trust us. We're here to keep you safe."

Lucky?

"Safe from what?" I manage to croak, a rogue tear slipping from my eye.

The man who caught me outside and guided me into the car reaches forward and with a slow and precise movement swipes the tear with the pad of his thumb from my cheek. His eyes are a blazing blue that seems to penetrate me to my core. I can tell he's the oldest in the group by the way he seems to drip with authority that makes me feel safe. My eyes linger on a rogue strand of inky-black hair that hangs over his dark brow. It makes me want to reach over and push it away so I have an unobstructed view of his gorgeous eyes.

"From the wolves trying to take a bite," he answers with a smile, his hand lingering on my skin a second longer than necessary. It's strange the instant calm saturating my body with them all watching me. "I'm Sebastian Constantine. I started IDS four years ago and brought in my most trusted ex-military brothers. Every single one of these guys, I trust with my life. And you can too, Miss Sterling."

"Clo is fine," I murmur.

Sebastian grins and then nicks his head toward the dark-haired brooding one on the other side of him. "You can trust us, *Clo*. Even this wise guy."

Ford snorts. "Zac? He's shady. You gotta watch him."

Zac, the man in question, turns his dark-brown eyes my way. His jaw clenches as though he's angry, which causes my pulse to quicken. Then, he winks at me. No smile or anything else, just a wink. It surprisingly calms me.

"Zac Stone," he grunts out. "Electronic Security Agent."

Sebastian leans forward again, capturing me with his electric blue eyes. "We are a team. *Your* team. Keeping people safe is our specialty. We won't let you down, Clo."

For the first time in a long time, fear ebbs inside me like a receding tide.

Not fear of being in danger, but the fear of being alone.

I sigh and relax back into the comfort of my seat, my eyes closing and exhaustion coming over me. For the first time in forever, I think I'll be able to sleep tonight.

They are here to save me from the big bad world.

I have my own four saviors.

And I need them, for future days like this.

I am not alone.

They are mine.

1

Clove Sterling—The Client

Six years later…

Image after image flits across my screen from William's Facebook page as I scroll through, stalking his profile. I don't even remember these photos of us being taken. It's like he has a version of our relationship in his mind that differs so much from reality it's worrying.

It's almost as if he's designing a picture-perfect illusion just for the outside world, which doesn't surprise me. I lived that way my whole life. It's something I've come to expect from the people in my life.

William, like my father, is in politics. Image is everything to them. Damn, him being like Dad was the appeal in the first place. Not in a creepy way, just in a *He's what I know* kind of way. What I've always been taught is normal. What was expected of me.

He's perfect according to my dad.

He should try dating him.

"Us" on paper is the perfect match, but chemistry doesn't take note of whom we should be attracted to and it dropped the ball on this one.

William is handsome, but he lacks sex appeal. We have sex on a schedule since I let him take my virginity four years ago on my nineteenth birthday. Everything I'd built up in my mind over the years was replaced with the reality of missionary style, five thrusts and it's over kind of sex. I'd been led to believe from TV shows that, that was supposed to happen years after marriage, not straight from the start. I didn't even feel the pain you're supposed to have when losing your virginity. It was just bland and over too quick to notice pain, or pleasure. I'd always been a sexual person, *with myself anyway.*

My fantasies had kept me company and created an expectation that William could never live up to.

I'm still not sure if it's normal or if there is something wrong with me, because I long to be tasted, to be touched for hours, in every place forbidden and otherwise. I want passion like you see in the movies or even the dirty, all positions sex that you see in porn videos.

The lust, the need, the raw, rough touch of a man who wants to devour me.

It's maybe because I've grown up in a household of men who all look like they walked from the pages of a fitness catalogue or straight off a movie set. My four guys set a high standard in the looks department.

I've had crushes on them since they walked into my life six years ago. They were the reason I bought my first vibrator. I'd been having naughty dreams about each of them and sometimes not separately for as long as I could remember. I'd ordered the toy online, then it became my best friend and probably the reason I didn't feel pain with William.

It isn't just that they're all handsome, though.

Each of my guys are also unique, offering something I've always needed. Attention. Affection. A listening ear. Protection. But above all of those…company.

Just knowing they are around, somewhere in the house, makes me feel less…alone.

I didn't have the typical upbringing, so friends were sparse and boyfriends weren't allowed until I turned eighteen, and even then, he was picked for me by Dad's security team. Background and social media check to make sure he was not only worthy but not some secret creep. Dates arranged and organized, my outfits chosen for me until I reached nineteen and grew a backbone. That was all thanks to Ford, who snort laughed at my cardigan one day. It had rabbits printed all over it and I looked five, not a nineteen-year-old woman ready to lose her virginity. Ford took me shopping that day, letting me try on anything I wanted. I changed my entire wardrobe that weekend and never looked back, much to Marjorie's horror. Apparently having a backbone also means you're a PR nightmare. I'm a good daughter, though, and play by her rules when it counts.

Clothes hold power. When I need to be who my father wants me to be, I can put on a skirt and blouse and pretend I'm that girl. When I'm feeling bold and want to shed that expectation, I can replace the blouse and skirt with a flirty dress and become more carefree. But best of all, when I need to feel special and sexy, I can be just me in lace underwear. William never once has taken off my bra during sex, which I find weird and wish I had someone close I could confer with. I'd say he never takes it off because my breasts look so appealing in the lacy number, but he always frowns when I wear sexy underwear. He told me that a lady doesn't wear items like that. He also told me it wasn't like girls to want sex.

I've always felt shamed by him.

I read up online that it's normal to have a high sex drive when you're young, but not sure if it refers to the person being single or in a relationship. Your hormones go crazy, the articles stated. Well, I'm twenty-three now and I'm still horny and frustrated.

Looking down at my left hand, I sigh deep. My thoughts are weighted with the information slipped to me by his sister. A proposal is coming. The thought of being married to William leaves a pit in my stomach growing wider each day. I can't marry him.

Things with William just won't work out. I can't keep fooling myself into thinking it will.

Just visiting him has become a chore and it's not fair to either of us to carry this on when we have the media's eyes on us all the time, creating a perfect couple when we're far from it.

I come to a picture of him with his family and sigh at the affection his mother's eyes hold as she looks up at her son adoringly. I miss my mom and yearn to be looked at with such affection.

Mom's death was six years ago, but the grief of it whenever I think of her is like salt being poured into a raw wound.

So much has changed since her death. She died in a car accident when Dad was running for governor. Instead of it stalling his career, it launched it. The media coverage and magazines all writing pieces on his strength and single fatherhood did wonders for his vote. But the truth was, his staff raised me. And when I say raised, I mean looked out for. I practically raised myself. Now he's heading for the White House and his time for me is less than before. I adore him, however, and he does me. I just wish our time together wasn't forced into his schedule. He's asked to meet with me for coffee at a local shop later, because finding time within our own walls is impossible.

He's hardly ever home and I just exist within the walls here. He wants to discuss his campaign and my role while he runs for president. Do I tell him that I don't want to have to be a part of the charade?

I check my cell phone and see I have a couple of hours to spare before meeting Dad, so I pull up William's contact.

Me: Can we meet this morning?

Five minutes later comes his reply.

William: I can pencil you in at 10:30 for half an hour?

His reply causes me to roll my eyes. I need someone to not have to pencil me in and be elated that I want to spend time with them.

I close the laptop and slip off my bed. It's hot, too hot, and the AC hasn't been working in my room for two days. Going to the window, I shove it up higher and suck at the air, trying to fill my lungs and cool my sweaty skin. I've been sleeping in just my panties and it's still been too hot. We're having an unusually hot fall. I can't wait for the cooler weather to roll in.

My eyes flutter closed and I take a minute to think about what I'm going to say to William.

"Hey, you don't satisfy me. We should break up."

"We need to talk. It's over. Bye."

"I'm insatiable and you hate fucking me, so it's over."

"William, you will always be a part of my..."

Ugh, lame.

I open my eyes and startle when my eyes clash with Sebastian's brilliant blues, the leader of Dad's security detail, standing in the yard. He and his team have worked for Dad exclusively since Mom's death, so he's no stranger to me, but the look in his eyes when they find mine is different to any other time he's seen me.

Shock at first. Then, intensity. Finally, hunger.

My brow furrows and it's then I realize I'm wearing just my underwear. The window is low and shows my entire torso to his focused gaze.

Crap!

Usually, the grounds at the back of the house are empty. It's just two miles of greenery. But not today. Today, Sebastian is out there, his cell phone to his ear and his blazing blue eyes glued on me.

Breathe, Clove. Breathe, Clove.

I can't breathe, though. My chest constricts squeezing my lungs, causing my eyes to bulge.

It takes me a few seconds to move away and pin my back to the wall beside the window, taking a huge gulp of air. My heart is racing and my hands are shaking, a thrill coursing through me that shouldn't be.

He didn't look away. He just stared at my exposed skin and that has an excitement pooling in my stomach that I don't understand. It was just an accidental situation, but my entire body is humming with need now. Manifesting and dampening my panties. *I'm not normal.*

I peek to see if he's still there, but he's not. The space he was standing in is now vacant. My heart deflates a little for no reason. *Did I make him up?*

I'm being stupid for liking the thrill of him seeing me nearly naked. Sebastian has always given me a pulse deep in my stomach. His authority mixed with those looks are a deadly combination and I've always had a feeling of fear and excitement when in his presence, like he could punish me if I ever broke the rules, but his punishment would be brutally sinful. I've imagined being put over his knee on more occasions than deemed sane.

Biting my lip, I check the time on my cell. Half past nine. I have time. Rushing over to my bed, I slip my pink toy from the bedside cabinet and shimmy my panties down my thighs, lying back and letting thoughts occupy my mind that shouldn't.

Visions of me doing this with him watching, with the other team members watching, have my back arching. I imagine my four guys surrounding my bed, each one touching themselves encouraging me, guiding me, commanding me. I let the vibrations dance over my clit as I fantasize that I'm on display for Sebastian and his whole team, spreading myself open for them, driving myself fucking crazy. They're all around my bed watching, but not allowed to touch. I open myself up more, exposing my glistening pussy to the room, and massage the pink tip over and over my bundle of nerves until my toes curl. Then, I slip it inside and clench around it as illicit ripples of pleasure wash over me.

It's fast when the orgasm hits, igniting every nerve in my body. My heavy pants fill the air and a smile creeps up my face.

Once the high cools and I slip the device from inside me, shame replaces it.

I'm not normal.

Getting turned on by someone I've known for years accidently seeing me? I'm desperate and pathetic.

William was supposed to take care of these needs and instead he just made me more frustrated.

A tapping at my bedroom door jolts me from my thoughts and I see the handle drop, so I scurry to pull my panties up, tossing the toy over the end of my bed and sitting up on my knees.

The door opens and Sebastian is standing there. All six feet and probably five inches of him. Solid frame. Scruffy cheeks, tense jaw, and narrowed eyes.

"Oh, sorry," he says in a husky voice, taking in my still undressed state and turning his broad back to me. My eyes widen and I grab a pillow to cover myself. I know my cheeks are burning from my afterglow and I look guilty because I am. Does he know? Will he be embarrassed for himself? For me?

"It's fine," I croak out.

He chances a glimpse over his shoulder, a feral glint in his eyes, and sees that I've covered myself before nodding and turns to fully face me again. "I'm sorry about before." He gestures toward the window and then rubs a hand over the back of his neck. *Is he blushing*?

I'm shaking my head before he's even finished the sentence. "No, it was my fault. For not putting clothes on." I laugh awkwardly and his eyes darken as they drag over me. "The AC is broken in here," I quickly add. "I just needed some air to circulate the room. It's so hot." I'm mumbling like an idiot. It's like I'm meeting him for the first time and haven't spent six years under this roof with him.

His tongue slips past his full lips, swiping out to taste the bottom one. "Yes, I can see that," he states, once again dragging his eyes over me like he can see through the pillow I'm clutching like a life raft.

I blush harder and bite on my bottom lip. I don't feel twenty-three. I feel like a virginal teenager under his observation. He moves farther into my room and toward the vent of my AC and my stomach drops. Sickness from humiliation explodes inside me when he rounds the bed and his foot kicks the vibrator I tried to get rid of. Time slows and I will the bed to cave in on itself with me inside it when his eyes drop to the offending item.

He's bending down as I'm scrambling forward off the bed. *No…no…no.*

He reaches it before I do, clasping it in his palm, and rises to his full height. I'm now standing in front of him, the pillow abandoned, and humiliation racing a red flush over my skin.

I snatch it from his hand and hide it behind my back like that will fucking erase the fact he saw it and touched it. He could probably see the sheen of my release over it. Smell me. Oh God, kill me.

He's staring at his hand, the one that was holding my used toy a second ago, and my eyes expand with worry that any juices may be on there.

"I'm mortified," I choke, my brows furling together and tears building in my eyes.

"We all have needs, Clo." He swallows and I'm transfixed on the movement in his throat. I always thought he resembled a vampire, but now *I* feel like one. Because I want to lean in and take a bite of the pulse jumping in his neck.

"Sebastian?" a bark comes from the doorway, making me almost leap from my skin. Turning my gaze to the offending voice, I see another member of his team, Ford, standing there looking in at us. Ford has always been a friend to me, but that tone isn't friendly. The room heats and I look between them both, praying Sebastian doesn't mention this incident to him.

"I was just checking the AC. It's broken in here," Sebastian rumbles.

If I'm not mistaken, he sounds guilty.

My skin burns, and dammit if I don't feel guilty too.

"Yeah, looks hot in here," Ford grunts and then the aggression from moments before disperses into his signature smirk, his eyes raking over my exposed body like it's telling him a story.

Holy shit. Twice in one morning another man has seen me in my underwear.

"We need to get ready. Zac wants to go over the plan for today," Ford informs him.

There's a silent pause in the room before we all start moving. I step over to the bed, pulling the sheet up to cover my front. Sebastian turns and heads for the door that now has Ford propped up against the frame, smiling in at us like he knows a secret that we don't. There's mischief in his features and I know he thinks he walked into more than what he actually did.

What would Dad think if I started something with a member of his security team?

He would fire them and forbid me from telling anyone so it didn't become a scandal that could tarnish our reputation. I can fantasize, though. No one has control over that.

I watch them leave and breathe out a shaky breath before slipping to the bathroom for a shower, taking my pink pleasure toy with me.

2

Ford Cross—Executive Weapons Specialist

Watching Sebastian grinding his jaw and trying to hide the bulge in his slacks as he rushed from Clove's room is one of the funniest things I've seen. The bastard has had a thing for her since she reached *fucking* age. We all have if the truth be told. He wouldn't admit it, though, but we've been best friends since we met in Afghanistan and worked together ever since. I know our team better than I know myself. I don't blame him for not admitting what she does to him. Clove is stunning. Like stupid hot with fucking curves most socialites have to pay a surgeon for.

She's the boss's daughter, though, so she's off-limits. That was Sebastian's rule when starting our company over a decade ago and it's never been a problem…until *her.*

We may know that she's off-limits, but sometimes, the little versions of us in our pants don't understand that shit, hence Sebastian trying to stop the blood pumping to his cock.

"Broken AC?" I snort.

"It was," he snaps back, and I hide my grin behind my hand as we approach the others.

"Why were you two with Clove?" Leo asks.

How the fuck did he know?

"I just went to get Sebastian," I defend, holding my hands up in mock surrender.

"Broken AC," Seb spits out, at the same time running a hand through his raven-colored hair and looking down at his feet to avoid eye contact.

Leo quirks a brow, his eyes darting between us. "What?"

"What?" we both say in unison with a shrug.

Shaking his head, Leo holds out his phone with a text showing from Clove.

Clove: I need to go to William's office this morning. Sebastian and Ford will accompany me. Please have the car ready in thirty minutes. Thank you. x

Well, shit.

"She doesn't usually see him on Mondays," Leo adds, his tone questioning.

"I'm not her keeper," I grunt. "I just keep her safe." I run a hand over the back of my neck and then over my head, messing up my gel. I need a haircut.

An awkward pause thickens the air. Leo has always been too interested in Clove's life. What she does and when. He's overprotective and it's nothing to do with her being a job or the fact he's in charge of gathering intelligence. He has feelings for her that go beyond his duty, and he's not good at hiding that fact or gives a shit that any of us know it. It can happen when you're around the same client for long periods of time.

Shit, calling her a client feels wrong. Less than what she truly is.

They're supposed to be just a job. Six years is a long

job, but still a job. Nothing more. But deep down, I have a hard time convincing myself. And lately, it's becoming harder to ignore, especially when she traipses around looking hot as fuck all the time.

Images of her in her underwear, a glow to her cheeks, plays on repeat in my head. Goddammit.

"Ford? You listening to me?" Sebastian barks, narrowing his accusing and sometimes creepy-fierce blue eyes at me. The fucker knows I wasn't listening and probably knows where my thoughts were.

Nodding, I focus my attention on him with a tight grin.

"You'll go with Zac and accompany him to the coffee meeting with Mr. Sterling. We'll show up with Clove." Zac prefers to be assigned to Clove's father's protection detail rather than hers for some fucking crazy reason. Why he'd choose Jack over Clove is beyond me. Watching over Clove feels more like a reward than a job.

Sebastian motions to the car. "We'll take the Bentley."

Sounds good.

Clove is dressed in a pencil skirt and blouse. A string of pearls hug her delicate neck and her long, dark brown hair is pulled up into a tight, neat bun. Lately, she wears this juicy as fuck gloss on her pouty pink lips that makes my mouth water for a taste. Her brown eyes are always made up with liner and mascara, but I prefer her when she's at home and scrubbed clean. Those honey brown eyes seem to pop and reveal more of the real Clove.

I feel like more and more, especially because of her being with her Ken doll William, she's lost the real Clove and had to be her dad's puppet for the press a little too often.

I'm not a fucking fan of Politician Daughter Barbie.

She always looks too put together these days. Seeing her in disarray this morning in just her underwear was enlightening, reminding me of the time I took her shopping when she asked me if she looked appealing in a sexual way years ago. She was wearing a stupid fucking sweater thing with animals all over it. She could pull anything off, but I knew she had never picked out her own clothes her entire life. So, I took her to the mall. It was like letting a caged animal free into the world. She went from shop to shop, happily choosing things she wanted, and finished up in a lingerie shop.

Lace. Lace fucking panties. I could give her a pearl necklace to match those and not the kind she has on now…

I shake her image from my thoughts for the hundredth time.

The body she hides beneath her clothes is deadly. She's a knockout. And the image won't leave my fucking mind no matter how many times I force it from it.

"I'm nervous," she announces, getting my attention for a whole other reason.

She's clenching her hands together and my shoulders stiffen.

I flit my eyes to Sebastian, who is driving for a change, and catch his eyes on her in the rearview.

"Why?" I ask, frowning. My gut coils with its own nerves of what she's going to say. I take her hand and give it a squeeze before releasing it.

"I'm going to break things off with William." She sighs and shifts in her seat next to mine.

We're used to her talking about her life with us. We're the people she sees the most of, so she's adapted and become open with some of us. Mainly Leo, who treats her like she's a breakable fucking doll, and me who just treats her like she's human. I think she'd surprise everyone just how unbreakable she is.

I'm so fucking relieved at her words. I had this image of her marrying that cocksucker.

"He's wrong for you anyway," I tell her boldly, ignoring the tightening of Sebastian's jaw.

Usually, I just listen to her and not actually intervene, but William doesn't deserve her. He treats her like she's an accessory. He only wants to take her out when it's a photo op for him. He's too much like her father. Clove needs a man who's devoted to her. She's a fucking catch, yet to this political bastard she's just a means to an end. He's trying to use her father's influence and fame for his own gain.

No one actually looks past her last name to see the woman standing right there before them. She's bright, beyond beautiful, and caring. Funny and sweet. Determined and focused.

"You really think that?" she whispers after a silent pause. For a moment, I worry I said that shit out loud, but then remember we were discussing William.

"I do. You deserve someone who demands your time. Who will go to the ends of the earth to make sure you're happy and satisfied." I nod. Her eyes grow wide at the mention of satisfied and it sends a flurry of visions through my head of being the one to satisfy her.

"We're here," Sebastian announces. I unbuckle both our seat belts and slip out of the car.

Sebastian is already out and at her door before I can get to it.

"You stay outside. I'll go in with her," he grunts.

With a nod, I check the streets and then take a stance outside the entrance to William's office building.

3

Clove Sterling—The Client

Fidgeting, I wring my hands together as the elevator climbs the building. Why is it so damn hot in here? Sebastian and I are the only two people inside the tin can and his pure size and closeness has me forgetting my nerves and instead the excitement in my stomach is back.

It's like my body has woken up after a long sleep. I sense every part of him in here with me. The rise and fall of his chest as he breathes, the trickle of sweat beading on his forehead, his hand accidently brushing the fabric of my clothes, his breath dispersing over my face as he looks down at me, the muscles flexing in his jaw. I'm going to combust.

Sebastian is in his early thirties, but it doesn't stop a heat that begins to flame up my neck with him this close. He's tall, well over six feet. Broad shoulders. Piercing blue eyes and the blackest hair that looks like spilled ink. The fierce glint that always flickers in his gaze reminds me of a vampire again, but it's me who is thirsty in here, not him.

I've watched too many movies. My imagination likes to go crazy from time to time. *Imagine if he really were a vampire and he bit me in* other *places?*

"You're looking flustered," he suddenly says and my eyes widen.

"I…erm." My tongue feels too big for my mouth.

A small tug of his lips and then he adds, "He will be fine. Besides, I'll be right outside if you need me." The elevator jolts to a stop and the door dings open.

"Thanks," I croak, moving as fast as possible out of the enclosed space.

I walk straight down the corridor and past Mary, William's secretary. She starts to stand, her hand waving in protest as she almost falls from behind her desk to reach me, but Sebastian stands in her way, blocking her approach.

"He's expecting me, Mary," I call around his large frame.

"I still need to announce you," she argues, but it's muted by the thickness of Sebastian's body between us.

I rap my knuckle on William's door and then push the handle to go inside. He looks up as I enter the room. There's a man sitting opposite him, who follows William's gaze to me. I drop my eyes to study him and swallow when his dark orbs narrow on me.

"Clove, you're early." William stands and runs his hand down his tie.

"Sorry, I'm actually five minutes late. I can come back another time if you're busy," I offer. But really, I won't make another appointment to see him. I'll just end things on the phone when he can slip a call in.

He's shaking his head vehemently and moving from foot to foot like he's anxious.

"Are you going to introduce us?" the other man says, rising to his feet, and comes toward me. The clothes he's wearing are unusual for this environment, which leads me to believe he's not here on business. Leather in the form of a jacket sits snug over his wide shoulders. A T-shirt pulls tight against his abdomen with a logo of a rock band emblazoned on the fabric. Jeans sitting low on his narrow hips travel down his legs and disappear into heavy black boots that stop just as the tip of his boot reaches the end of my stiletto.

The urge to move back is suffocating, but I refuse to be intimidated, and that's the vibes coming off this man. His eyes are narrowed and a sneer lifts his lip as he states, "You've been moving up in the world. She's an improvement from the last one."

Just as my mouth opens to tell him to back away, a large hand reaches around my waist and tugs me backward against a hard chest. Sebastian's scent surrounds me as his other powerful hand reaches forward and pushes against this man's chest.

"You're too close," Sebastian growls in warning.

I feel the heat and grip of his hold in more places than my waist and I fight the urge to inhale him and sink back into his powerful body.

"It's okay," William intervenes, pulling me from my fuzzy thoughts, finally coming around his desk and grabbing the man's arm to step around him. He's not looking at me but at the giant behind me, who's protecting me. "She's fine," he tells Sebastian without asking me if I'm indeed fine. In his hold, I feel more than fine.

"This is a school friend of mine from a long time ago. He's just visiting and now leaving." William glances over his shoulder and the guy smirks with a shoulder shrug.

"No offense intended." He holds up his hands in surrender.

"You can release her now," William urges, but Sebastian doesn't release me, merely relaxes his hold slightly, which I'm grateful for because my knees have weakened.

"Actually, this was just a quick visit to let you know in person that this"—I gesture between him and me—"isn't working. I have another engagement to get to so…" I know I sound discombobulated, but I can't think straight through the Sebastian haze.

Pull yourself together, I scorn internally.

William's jaw is slack and his pale blue eyes widen in shock. He should be enough, he should be better at the things I need, but he's just not.

"You're joking?" He chortles, running his fingers through his blond hair. But the laughter fades when he realizes I'm not smiling. It's not a joke.

"Clove? You can't end us. We're perfect together. Our careers—"

I hold a hand up to stop him. He means *his* career. I do charity work. I'm not trying to climb rungs of a ladder like William. His ego gives me the ammo I need to clear the haze of sexual chemistry I seem to be consumed with today.

"*Your* career. Being with you does nothing to further my own agenda, just yours," I bite out.

"I love you," he tries.

His friend from school, who's still standing behind him, barks out a laugh, gaining all our attention. With hands going up in surrender, he says, "Sorry, carry on."

What a rude sonofabitch. I should have waited for him to leave. Picked another time to do this, but if I wait, it's just prolonging the inevitable.

"You love the idea of me," I mutter. "There's a difference."

William's jaw locks and the muscles tick there. He places his hands on his hips as he paces the floor. Sebastian's hold has loosened, but he hasn't fully let me go.

"Can we talk about this at a more appropriate time? It's hardly the place, Clove."

"Will I just book another time slot to see you then?" I bite out.

"I don't give you enough time. I can do better," William says with a resigned sigh.

"Do better with the next woman who comes into your life." I reach out for him and squeeze his arm, before turning on my heel and coming face-to-face with Sebastian's chest. He stands in my way for a beat too long before stepping aside and letting me pass.

Just as I get through the door I turn back. "It was nice meeting you…?"

"Ren. Ren Hayes." The friend smirks.

"*The* Ren Hayes?" Sebastian stiffens, causing me to go on alert.

William pales and slams the office door shut in Sebastian's face.

"Rude," I snap out.

"Come on," Sebastian urges with his hand to the small of my back, sending shock waves up my spine and liquid heat to pool in my stomach.

We don't speak again until we're back in the car. This time Ford takes the driver's seat and Sebastian joins me in the back.

I unbutton a couple buttons on the blouse I'm wearing. I'm flustered and mad at how things went up there in

William's office. And, like a bitch in heat with every touch or look from Sebastian, despite knowing him for over six damn years, it only worsened things. Ugh. These professional clothes are a hindrance. I can't breathe. I'd love to put on my shorts and tee and just feel normal for once.

To feel free.

"What did you mean, *The* Ren Hayes?" I turn to ask Sebastian to distract myself, but the question fades when I find his eyes on the cleavage I've exposed. My heart rate quickens and water floods my mouth.

"Ren Hayes?" Ford barks over his shoulder. "The man just acquitted for the murder of that woman from that club? It was on the news."

All heat drains from my body, leaving an icy chill in its wake. I look at Sebastian for confirmation and going from the dip in his brow and tense posture, I'd say that's exactly who he meant.

"Drive," Sebastian demands.

I flop back into my seat, not realizing I'd darted forward when Ford brought up just who I was toe to toe with minutes before. *Murder?*

Death's cold hand snakes up my spine, whispering over the flesh, causing goose bumps to rise all over my skin. Sebastian shifts in his seat, his thigh coming to rest against mine, reminding me I have nothing to fear from Ren or men like him. Because I have four protectors who won't allow anyone to harm me.

4

Sebastian Constantine—Chief Protection Specialist

Anxious energy has been coursing through my veins ever since we left William *small dick's* office.

Fucking Ren Hayes was the last person I wanted around Clo and the fact he was in William's office with William working for the state is foolish of him. That's a media storm just waiting to happen.

The boring bastard looked twitchy as fuck and with good reason if he has a past linked with Ren Hayes. Ren was accused of the murder of a woman named Kate Rose. She met him at a nightclub and was later found strangled to death. Ren's DNA was found on the victim and his fingerprints on a silk scarf wrapped around her neck. He claimed they were an item before she died, and were into rough sex. And that the scarf was a gift he bought her.

But there was no evidence they were an item. The bastard charmed the jurors and got off.

Lack of evidence.

Now I'm on edge. We looked into William when they first started dating, but this business with Ren came later. He wouldn't have flagged up. I will be doing a fresh look into William's background when we get done with this coffee meeting with her father.

⇝⋄⇜

Zac and Leo arrived at the coffee house with Mr. Sterling a few minutes ago. He's decided to sit outside, which makes our job of keeping them safe twice as hard. Crowd points of possible attacks are greater in open space. But Mr. Sterling likes to be seen. It's good for his image.

I search the perimeter of the coffee shop again and nod to Ford, who sits next to the table Clo and her dad are having coffee at. It's apparent he only wanted to meet in a public space when the paparazzi show up and begin snapping them together. Jack Sterling needs the world to think he's a devoted father spending time with his only child. We all know better. Clo would never see him if it wasn't good for his image. I'm not saying he doesn't love or care for her, he just loves his career more. It's been fucking tough watching her grow into this beautiful woman, but so lonely and in desperate need of love.

It's all around her, yet she can never know it.

I can't hear what they're talking about, but the quick glimpses I give Clo tell me it's something she's not happy about—no doubt informing her of more photo shoots and organized events she will be required to attend. This girl never complains about being a tool in her father's campaigns. She does what's expected of her, like a puppet on a string. I'm dying to cut her loose from them, to set her free…or use them to string her up in more fun ways. Fuck, I need to stop thinking about her this way. She doesn't fucking help my cause. There's so much inside her waiting to burst free. I can see it battling under the surface, clawing for an escape, begging for me to unlock the cage she's kept in.

I used to love my job, the thrill of possible danger at any turn, but now, now I care so much about the girl I'm protecting I hate it. It stresses me out knowing there's always potential danger just by her having the Sterling name. Keeping her safe is something I vow to do no matter what, but I wish it were under different circumstances, that she was mine. That it didn't have to be from afar.

I'd give anything to just taste her. To feel her against my skin, her breath against my lips before I stole the air from her and made the world disappear with a kiss she'd never get from fucking *William*. Anything for one taste.

Leo checks his watch and nods over to me, refocusing my attention. It's been thirty minutes, which is plenty of time to make a good impression. Like clockwork, they finish up. He didn't even feed her.

"Leo, take Clove home. Sebastian, you and the others will go with me," Mr. Sterling informs us. Usually he leaves it for me to decide the protection detail arrangements, but he knows Clo likes Leo's company and going from her downturned lips, the meeting upset her.

I want to argue, but there's no reason Clo wouldn't be safe with Leo. He adores her and is as well trained as the rest of us.

I nod in confirmation and watch as Clo saunters over to Leo and gestures to the park across the street. She's always had a thing for walking. She loves nature and rarely gets to experience it.

As I turn away from her, I feel it in my bones before anything else. The atmosphere shifts and acid pools in my gut as I hear a car revving, the tires squealing and burning asphalt.

My heart stops as the world slows. I turn just in time to see Clo as she steps into the road, the car barreling toward her. But instead of slowing, it speeds up. A fucking rock forms in my throat, but I manage to bark, "Leo!"

Fear swells up inside of me as I race toward her. Leo must have seen the car already because he's pushing her out of the way and catches a clip to the leg as the car makes impact, sending him to the ground. I whip out my Glock, drawing it within a second.

My eyes are everywhere—checking the surroundings—dropping to see Ford aiding Clo.

"She's okay," he shouts, his own gun in hand.

Zac has ushered Jack inside the shop to keep him safe. Flashes spark from all the paparazzi taking shots of the incident. I aim at the car disappearing into the distance, but it's too risky to open fire with so many civilians around. Someone could get injured in the crossfire.

My chest is tight as I take in Clo crying into Ford's chest. My entire body is vibrating with a mix of nerves and rage. Someone tried to hurt—no, not hurt, fucking kill our girl.

Ford gathers Clo into his arms and carries her to the car we arrived in.

Motherfuckers.

Who the hell would want to hurt her?

Whoever they are, they're going to die.

5

Clove Sterling—The Client

Leave.

He wants me to leave.

My father blurs before me as tears well in my eyes. I don't understand why he wants me to go in the first place. I'm safest with him. With our security team. *My guys.*

And yet here he is demanding I flee.

"Dad," I beg. "Don't do this. We can find a safe house for both of us. No one will ever find us." It's been hours since the incident and I've been shaking ever since.

My father's brows furl together. Normally, he's smiling and jovial around me, but this has spooked him. Not just him. Tonight, he's anything but playful. "Someone tried to kill you, Clove," Dad growls. "They will try again. We need you safe until I can figure out who's behind this. If I'm too busy worrying over your safety, I won't be able to do that. I need to focus."

Marjorie materializes from the corner, her blond curls bouncing, and walks over to my dad. She grips his bicep and gives him a sad smile. It's embarrassing how completely and obviously into him she is. Dad is still not over Mom after six years. Poor Marjorie is chasing a lost cause.

"Your team is capable," Marjorie assures him. "Sending her away can't possibly be the answer."

I nod rapidly in agreement. We may not always see eye to eye on our clothing choices and how I hold myself in front of the public, but she's definitely on my team.

Dad pats her arm and shakes his head. "No, she needs to go. We'll keep it out of the media. You can do this for me."

Her lips purse together and I can tell she wants to argue, but in the end, she flutters her fingers over his in an affectionate, comfortable way before nodding and sentencing me to this new destiny.

"Sir," Sebastian growls. "Time is of the essence."

Dad frowns and pulls me to him. "I love you, baby girl. Give me time. I'll sort all of this out in no time at all. Then, I'll come back for you. In the meantime, go with my team. They'll keep you safe." He's sending me with his team?

"But who will keep *you* safe?" I demand through my tears. I'm worried someone will come and take him away from me. I've already lost my mom. I can't lose him too.

"Advanced Security," Sebastian grunts. "They're more than capable."

I turn and frown at him.

"Clove," my father urges because I'm stuck staring at Sebastian inventing a make-believe world where we're not in imminent danger and he didn't just suggest we leave my dad without his protection.

"More than capable isn't good enough," I snap, unfairly taking out my emotions on Sebastian. My body is at war with my head. I just want to run to him and make him hold me. But I can't do that. He's not really mine, no matter how much I pretend each one of them are.

"He needs the best. He needs you." I swallow past the pebble in my throat.

Sebastian's eyes flare and I get a flicker in my mind of him rushing toward me and taking a bite out of my neck. I rub my hand there without thought.

"No," Dad corrects. "*You* need the best. That's why I'm sending IDS."

"I won't go," I argue, crossing my arms over my chest. I know I'm being a brat, acting like a child and not the woman I am, but he is all the family I have left.

Dad kisses the top of my head before whispering, "I'm sorry." He pushes me toward Sebastian. "Go."

"Wait!" I cry out, but it's too late. Sebastian is on me, his powerful arms pulling me against him. I start to protest more, but his hand slaps over my mouth, silencing me. *Bastard.*

My legs kick out on instinct and try to make purchase, to no avail.

"Shhh," Sebastian murmurs, his hot breath at my ear sending a wave of emotions through me I refuse to admit to. "Try not to make a scene in case anyone is watching."

Who would be watching when we're in *our* home?

Silent tears stream down my face, but I stop fighting him. It's done. The decision has been made by my father and there's no changing it. Sebastian easily totes me through our massive kitchen, and into the garage. My other three guys all turn to regard us as we come through the door.

The four of them are everything to me after my father, and I just want to evaporate into them and allow them to absorb me. They've been here with us since I was seventeen. Absolutely trusted by my father, by me. And

I love them all dearly. I sniffle against Sebastian's hand still wrapped over my mouth as I come to terms with my fate. It's me and them now. I relax back against Sebastian, the leader and the fiercest of all of us, enjoying the hard planes of his body. His right-hand man is Leo, who regards me with a deep frown. Where Sebastian is tall, dark, and handsome, Leo is younger and built like some Roman god who normally seems to glow. Not tonight, though. Tonight, Leo is scowling and seems agitated at my distress. It makes me want to squeal and beg him to help me stay, help me keep Dad safe. Instead, I plead with my eyes before dropping them to his injury. His leg took some damage from the car that tried to run me down like roadkill. It's bandaged from knee to ankle and a fresh tear slips from my eye. He could have been killed saving me.

Following my gaze, his frown lines smooth out and he shrugs. "I haven't had time to change. It doesn't hurt, Clove," he says, with a quirk of his lips. "I'm a tough cookie."

I mumble against Sebastian's palm, but it's too muffled to make sense.

"You don't have to hold her so tight," Leo snaps, prowling our way. "Right, Clo?"

I blink and more tears slide down my cheeks, soaking Sebastian's palm.

"That's what I thought," he coos. "Come here. I'll take care of her in the car. Seb, you navigate us where we need to go."

"We driving the Tahoe?" Zac asks, his dark brown eyes sharp and alert. Where the other two men are solid and bulked with muscle, Zac is tall and lean like a runner. He never smiles at me like the others do. Zac is always tense and agitated, as though he's a rubber band ready to snap at any moment. He recently just celebrated his thirty-second birthday. Hiking or something. When I noticed his absence, Ford informed me he took a week off to celebrate alone in the wilderness. I can't even imagine what being alone in the wilderness would entail.

"Tahoe is all gassed up," Leo says as he pulls me to his warm chest, safely away from Sebastian. He strokes my hair and it makes the guilt burrow deeper. I should be taking care of him.

Why is this happening? I'm harmless. Killing me would be pointless. It makes no sense.

"I don't want to leave my dad," I whisper against his suit jacket.

"I know, sweetness. But we have to. It's not permanent. Just a temporary safe place," he assures me as he guides me over to the Tahoe.

Zac stands beside the vehicle and opens the door. His dark eyes flare with an emotion that I might equate to anger. I think he's mad because he's stuck babysitting me. But before I can worry myself over it, he winks at me, which serves to soothe my guilt of dragging them away to God knows where.

"Everything will be just fine, Clove," Zac says. "Just let us take care of you. It's our job."

I want to argue and tell him his job is taking care of my dad, and to have save lives, specifically my father's considering where his career is headed. But Leo is already gripping my hips and hoisting me into the Tahoe. His touch, so tender yet protective, warms me, making my stomach dip and body relax. Now is not the time to acknowledge the feelings I harbor toward Leo or any of the others.

"Come here, Lucky," Ford says, already seated inside the vehicle.

I scramble across the seat to bury my face against his chest. Ford is never without a panty-melting smile. His hazel eyes are warm and inviting. And he always acknowledges me. Whereas Sebastian and Zac tend to respect my father, and not chat it up with his daughter, Ford and Leo choose to ignore the unspoken rules. Leo tends to be my security blanket. But Ford? Ford is my entertainment. He always has time for me. To make me laugh or to take me shopping or to ask me about my day. At thirty-one and the youngest at IDS, he's closer to my age than my dad's, and for some reason that makes me feel closest to him than anyone.

"I'm scared," I admit to him, tilting my head up to look at his beautiful face. His mess of dark, chocolate-colored hair that's always styled in that sexy just-fucked way is extra tempting tonight. Often, I've wanted to touch his hair, but I've never had the courage. If he or any of them rejected me, I'd lose them and they're my family.

He cups my cheek with his massive palm, and I sigh into it, allowing myself his affection. "You never have to be frightened when you're with us. We'll always take care of you, Lucky. You know that."

I smile at the nickname he gave me when he first met me six years ago. My entire world is tipping on its axis. The future feels uncertain. It makes me want to pounce on opportunities I've let slip by in the past. Which is why I don't stop myself from reaching up and touching his soft brown hair.

His smile falls and his hazel eyes harden, making my chest constrict. I'm stunned by his sudden expression change. He drops his gaze to my lips before looking away so abruptly it makes me startle. His jaw clenches as though he's angry with me. The butterflies in my stomach turn into mosquitoes draining the blood from me.

"Seat belt," Sebastian barks as he leans in inside the vehicle, making me tense from the sudden intrusion of sound. He snags the belt and crosses it over my chest like I'm a child. His arm brushes against my breasts, however, causing me to gasp involuntarily in surprise. Our eyes meet and I'm set alight by the blaze in his bright blue orbs. I can't look away. I'm caught in his intense gaze and my nipples ache from the small accidental touch. I'm not going to survive being alone with them. I just know it. My desperate need to be touched must show all over my face based on the way my skin burns with heat, creeping up my neck and over my cheeks for him to see and dissect.

He grips my jaw with his powerful hand and stares at me. "It's okay, Clo," he promises.

As soon as he pulls away, I miss the intense moment, the small touch, and his eyes on me. Something in his words tells me he means more than just the predicament. *It's okay, Clo. It's okay to get turned on when I touch you.*

He shuts the door and Ford leans closer to me. I'd been so engrossed in Sebastian's gaze I'd almost forgotten we weren't alone. Ford's body nudges up next to mine. The heat coming off him scorches a trail up my thigh. My adrenaline must be causing this sudden bout of hormones because everything feels too hot, too intense, too much. Ford watches me curiously as Sebastian climbs into the passenger's seat and Zac gets in the driver's seat. Leo climbs in on Ford's side and settles in the last row behind us.

I catch my father staring at us from the doorway. Powerful and fierce. He's in his element when he's leading people and making deals happen. I can tell he's confident in his decision by the way he watches us reverse out of the garage. Dad is right. He's scrappy. Advanced Security is just as good as IDS and Dad doesn't always need protecting.

Not like me.

I've never left home. Not for long anyway. I grew up with the finest in-home tutors. All the friends I had were children of his influential business associates chosen for me by Marjorie. Even my college courses were taken online from home. Dad didn't want me going off to college because of bad decisions that could happen there. He meant the party life that some socialites pick over their courses.

I've never made bad decisions that may affect my father's career. I've always been obedient and given him anything he's asked. So, to have this threat against my life, I'll do as I'm told once again because the truth is, I'm terrified.

A warm hand clutches my shoulder from behind and Leo peeks over the back of the seat. My nerves have me taking his hand and gripping it with my left one.

"Sleep now, sweetness," he rumbles, his words making my blood hum in my veins.

"Sleep," Ford agrees, reaching out to grab my right hand. "Let us take care of you."

As if their words hold magic powers a yawn forces its way out of me.

I close my eyes to attempt to rest, but I'm hyper aware of the way both Leo and Ford hold my hands. Without looking at them I know their eyes are on me. I will sleep to come, but it's impossible with Ford's hand clutching my own resting on my thigh close to my heat. It makes me shiver and naughty thoughts race through my mind. Ford starts to pull away and it's like my leg enjoys the attention because I move my knee over, so that my leg is pressed against his. My legs are parted, but my skirt still covers me.

Peeking my eyes open, I chance a look at Ford. His gaze is now forward and the oncoming headlights light up his features in the dark vehicle, making him seem like some sort of wicked entity. It makes me shiver. He confuses my action with being cold because he releases my hand to palm my thigh just below the hem of my skirt. Back and forth, he rubs my flesh to warm me up. Slowly and softly. It maddens me. Heat floods through me and I grow dizzy.

Just like all the silly romance movies I indulge in over the weekends.

But unlike those stories, he doesn't slide his hands up and explore me further. Eventually, I give up hope that he'll touch me and let sleep steal me away.

6

Sebastian Constantine—Chief Protection Specialist

I can tell the moment she falls asleep. I'm that in tune with the girl. I always have been. My connection goes back to the day she cried out after a nightmare. We'd recently received a threat against her father, Jack, and I'd panicked thinking they'd gotten into the house. I stormed into her bedroom. She sat on her knees in the middle of her bed, her nightgown pushed up her thighs, and her big brown eyes wide with fear. At eighteen, she was too damn beautiful for her own good. If she were my daughter, I would've locked her away in the goddamn wine cellar and thrown away the key.

But she's not my daughter. Fucking far from it.

That night, I went to her and cupped her pretty face in my palm. The moment I touched her skin, I could almost smell her sweet scent. Hell, I could practically taste it. And the allure it had on me was far too dark and depraved. She was so out of my reach, yet I craved to touch her anyway. It was then that I began to notice every detail about her.

I became obsessed. Craving her like nothing before. The fucking forbidden apple, juicy sweet…illicit.

Now, after actually smelling her precious cunt on the

toy she used to pleasure herself with earlier today, I'll never get her free from my mind. She imprinted herself there. I'm her prisoner.

"Where to?" Zac asks, stealing my attention from the sleeping angel in the backseat.

"Upstate. The woods," I grunt out. My men and I speak in code. Even though we were meticulous in our inspection of the Tahoe, you can never be too sure. There could be bugs and I'd rather not inform the enemy of our destination if they happen to be listening.

"Settle in," Zac says. "Get some sleep because I don't feel like we'll be doing much of that once we get there."

I know he means because we'll be on constant watch over sweet little Clove Sterling, but my mind goes *there*. The same place it goes whenever I jerk off to release tension. Her. Always her. So many times, since that night I touched her soft cheek, I've watched her. No longer as a protective paternal figure. Instead, I watch her with lust. An intense craving I'll never be able to sate. I notice the way her dresses curve over her perky tits and the way the hem falls above her knees, showing off her creamy skin that was meant to be tasted and adored.

I steal a look at her in the backseat. She's turned some in her seat and her leg is hooked over Ford's knee. His hand grips her thigh in a possessive way that makes me want to take her other knee and spread her sweet thighs open for us. Her skirt has ridden up and in the dark of the vehicle, I can make out the white flash of her lace panties beneath her skirt. It's not a pencil skirt like earlier since that one got dirtied up after the incident. Instead, she's changed into one with a loose fabric that rides up her legs with every movement she makes. My cock thickens, causing me to re-adjust myself.

"Don't," Zac mutters only for me to hear.

He means stop fucking obsessing. But I can't. I've gotten drunk a few times over the past four years and spilled my woes to him. How if life were different, I'd make a girl like her mine. Once, I went as far as to detail out every single thing I'd do to her tight cunt. All with my tongue. He left with a hard-on and told me to get in line. If she couldn't be his—theirs—then she couldn't be mine, so to let it go.

But I can't.

I fucking can't.

"I wish one of us from IDS could have stayed," Zac grumbles. "I don't trust those bastards from Advanced Security."

"Those Advanced guys are every bit as trained and capable as the four of us. They will do their job just as you would. Quit your bitching," I grumble.

None of us would have wanted to stay knowing the others got to disappear with Clo.

I steal another look at her. Her soft, dark brown hair hangs in silky waves in front of her shoulders and her plump lips are parted as she sleeps. Fuck, what I wouldn't give to suck on her bottom lip.

"She's fine." Ford rolls his eyes.

I twist further in my seat to get a good look at him. I don't like the smug look on his stupid face as he caresses her thigh. He's leaned back, his legs parted, in an easy way that suggests cuddling with Clo is a common situation. And for as often as he takes her out to do errands and stuff, I wouldn't be surprised if he managed to sneak in some closeness with her. With his narrowed hazel eyes on me, he delicately inches his fingers up along her bare thigh.

My hands fist and my nostrils flare. "Watch it," I warn.

He smirks. "She likes it."

"I will fucking kill you," I whisper through gritted teeth. If I don't get to touch her neither should he.

Ford lifts a brow and continues his lazy teasing on her skin. Even in the dark, I can tell his erection is about to burst from his slacks. There's no fucking way I can drive five hours with this prick pushing my buttons when it comes to her. He's letting me know things have changed. No more dancing around the fact things are different, she's different. She's not a job, she's our girl. One we all protect, take care of, and someone we want to be with. Some prick tried to take her from us. It changes a person—the situation. Feelings, when you nearly lose the one thing you realize you've been living for, become more. They become real, present, and need to be explored.

Who are we without her?

I don't fucking know anymore.

It's been too long. Everything, for the past six years, has revolved around her. She started as a job, but from the first tear I swiped from her apple red cheek, she ensnared us all. Enchanted us with her need for our protection. She needed us more than anyone ever has, and in more ways than we've ever allowed ourselves to admit. We belong to her and she to us.

"What's the plan?" Zac asks, distracting me from imagining all the ways I'm going to skin Ford alive. I want to be the one caressing her thigh or at least be close enough to watch her chest rise and fall as he does it.

I twist back in my seat and stare ahead at the lonely black highway. "Just get us there alive. Secure the property. Keep her safe."

"And then?"

"Then we wait. You know the drill."

"For how long?"

"As long as it takes."

7

Clove Sterling—The Client

I must have faded out and fallen asleep because I wake to someone carrying me in the dark. At first, I panic until I realize it's Leo carrying me from the Tahoe into a small cabin-like house. Everything is pitch-black aside from the moon shining through the thick trees, so it's hard to make it out properly.

"It's secure," Ford says. "Place is fucking small as hell, though."

Leo walks past him and up a set of rickety steps that creak under our weight. His feet thud against wood as we enter a darker space. It smells musty and old. Nothing like my expensive home back in the city.

"One bedroom with a bed and a sofa in the corner of the room in there," Zac grunts from already inside in a dark corner, gesturing toward an open door. "Not much else. Tomorrow, we can make a list of supplies. Tonight we make do."

Leo walks me into the bedroom and sets me down on a lumpy bed. It feels good to stretch out, though. I'm covered with a soft blanket I recognize the feel of from home. It's chilly in the house. I grumble at the unfairness as I was dying of heat just this morning. With it being October, the days still get hot, but the nights cool off really quick.

"I'm fucking beat," Ford gripes. "Some of us didn't sleep on the way here."

"Fuck off," Leo bites back.

Sheesh, tempers are flaring.

"There's room if you want to lie down," I offer. "I don't bite."

Seb growls from somewhere else in the dark room, reminding me that maybe he does bite. I shiver again.

"We'll take shifts. Two in here with her at all times," Seb agrees. "Zac, you take the sofa and Ford can sleep on the floor next to Clo. Leo and I will keep watch in the front room. At daybreak, we'll switch off."

The men shuffle around and then someone curses. Then, the bed sinks down and Ford's familiar scent envelops me.

"I don't sleep on floors," he tells me, his voice playful.

I bite back a laugh as he settles beside me. I'm cold and heat seems to radiate from him. Selfishly, I scoot closer to steal his warmth. He's stiff at first when I slide my leg over his thigh and curl against him, but he eventually relaxes. I rest my palm on his hard stomach before letting out a sigh.

The couch squeaks as Zac sits on it and shuffling feet can be heard as the other two men step out of the room. My mind flits back to this morning when someone tried to mow me down. Just thinking about it causes me to shudder.

"You okay?" Ford asks.

"Yep," I rasp out.

"Good. Sleep, babe."

I quiver at the sentiment but try to obey. It takes a while and I finally start to drift off.

I try to climb over Ford, but he senses my movements just as I have one leg over his waist and my butt skimming over his groin. His hands grip hold of my arms and he tenses. The blue hue of the moonlight shining in on us from a small window in the room lights his face and the look in his eyes steals my breath.

"What are you doing?" he croaks, his voice strained.

"I need..."

"You need what?" he almost pleads, his grip tightening on my arms. I can't help it. The sensations pooling in my gut have my ass dropping down on him. His growing erection sits in the crease of my ass cheeks and we both gasp at the contact.

"Lucky," he grunts, his brows furling and jaw tightening. "What are you doing?"

"She needs to pee," Zac suddenly snaps from beside the bed. I look up into his glare and shame washes over me. I'm acting whorish and reckless. These are the same men I've been around for years. As much as I want them to be *my* guys, in reality, they're employees of my father. And men, real men. They're not the soft, passive Williams of the world. They are fiery and masculine and feral. And way out of my league. I need to control myself.

"Come," Zac barks.

Oh God. "What?" I almost salivate.

"Come on. I'll show you where the bathroom is."

Oh, of course that's what he meant.

I slip my hand into one of his he's offering and he steadies me as I climb over Ford, who hisses when my foot grazes his hard-on as I slide from the bed. Quickly, I slide on my shoes.

The floor thuds under our feet as we leave the room, coming into a small living space where Sebastian and Leo are sitting at a four-chair dining table.

"What's going on?" Sebastian asks, rising to his feet, his piercing blue eyes alert and wary.

"She needs to pee," Zac answers for me.

Leo flinches and scratches at his neck. "Yeah, about that…"

"What? There is a bathroom, right?" I jest, rolling my eyes.

Seb and Leo exchange looks before Leo stands. He pulls open the blinds covering a window.

"The woods?" I gape.

"No." Sebastian tries to hide the amusement in his tone but fails. "But it is outside."

"Why the fuck is it outside?" Zac demands.

"Because this place is old as shit, and all places up here were built with outhouses."

I shift from foot to foot to try and alleviate the need to empty my bladder, but it just makes me need it more.

"Come on, I'll take you," Leo offers.

I look up at Zac and he shrugs. "I'll piss in a bush."

Leo takes my hand and leads me outside. The cold chill rips over my skin, chasing a shiver through my blood. "Want my jacket?"

"No, it's fine," I tell him with confidence and assurance. But it's not fine. I'm outside to pee. I'm not a diva type, but I'm also not used to *the great outdoors* living aspect of being out here in the woods.

We round the small building and come to a tiny wooden shack-like structure. Leo pushes the door open and gestures with his hand at the toilet inside. It's like a stall you'd see in a public bathroom, but way creepier and old. "No way." I shake my head vehemently, snatching my hand from his and folding my arms over my chest.

"Just don't think about it." He shrugs.

My mouth drops open. "There's no light. It's like an upright coffin. I can't go inside there," I protest.

"It's either in there or out there." He nods to the tree line where Zac is perched up against a tree relieving himself.

Dammit.

"I'm not closing the door," I grumble.

Leo chuckles and holds up his hands. "That's fine. Leave it open. I'll turn around so you keep your dignity." He smirks as I squint my eyes at him.

Taking a couple of steps inside, I cringe at the dark space. I can't see the condition of the seat in this light, but I'm betting it's as run-down as the house. I turn to see Leo watching me.

"Ready?" he asks with a smile in his tone.

"I guess I have to be." Lifting my skirt, I shimmy my panties down and try to hover over the seat without touching the walls with my hands or seat with my butt. I should do my squats because this is hard work.

"I don't hear anything," Leo calls out.

"It's being stubborn."

His frame shakes a little and then I watch his head dip before hearing the distinct sound of a zipper opening. Two seconds later, the sound of him relieving his bladder coaxes my own to relax. A sigh passes my lips as I relax.

Just as I'm finishing, something drops on the top of my head. It's big and moving.

A scream rips from my lungs as I bolt forward, my hands swatting at my hair. My panties are still at my knees and restrict my movements, causing me to tumble forward and hit the ground.

Leo is on me in seconds, trying to calm me down and assess the situation. In a flash, Zac is by his side, his features contorted with worry. "What happened?" he rushes out, looking all around me.

"Something was on me!" I cry out.

Heavy footfalls pound the ground until Ford and Sebastian are standing around me also, all four men looking down at me, scanning my body.

"There!" Ford shouts, pointing to something near my head. His foot lifts and comes down. "Spider." He grins.

Yuck. A spider?

"Good job, hero." Sebastian rolls his eyes at Ford in mockery.

I barely suppress a shudder just thinking about that thing crawling in my hair.

"Can you help me up?" I croak, my cheeks burning with humiliation.

Leo reaches down and gets me to my feet. My panties drop to my ankles and all four sets of eyes follow their trail.

Perfect.

I lift my foot to slip out of them because I'm pretty sure I peed on them and myself in my escape from the predator in the toilet. Before I can lean down and pick them up Zac does.

Oh my God.

"They're wet," he announces like it's normal for this to happen. This is so far from normal. I'm about to combust as my entire body goes into a hot ball of mortification. And did Sebastian just groan?

"I got scared and ran," I snap, defending the cause of the wetness. It's the pee. I'm sticking with that.

"Fell," Leo corrects. I hit my fist into his arm and he chuckles.

I hold my hand out to Zac, but instead of handing me back my panties, he walks off with them still clutched in his hand.

Erm…

"Where the fuck you going with those?" Seb barks, asking the question I couldn't.

"Wouldn't be the first pair of hers he's stolen," Ford jests.

My eyes widen. "What?"

"Nothing," Seb growls. "He's joking."

Ford snorts, making me squirm. I tuck a strand of hair behind my ear and look at the ground because this is information I would have never expected of Zac. Was it a joke? It had to be a joke. Why would he want my panties? I've seen the women fawn over him in the past. He could have anyone's panties.

"Let's get inside," Seb orders. "Dawn's breaking and Leo and I need some shut-eye."

We go inside and Ford groans from beside me as we pass the front door. I follow his line of sight to my panties hung over the fireplace being dried by the fire.

"I'm going to need some clothes. You didn't even let me pack a bag," I point out with a frown.

Leo strokes his hand down my back to comfort me. "We needed to get you out of town as soon as possible. We don't know how big this threat is."

Sebastian yanks off the shirt he's wearing and tosses it on one of the chairs. My eyes greedily skim over taut skin and ripped muscles. I gulp as I follow the trail of dark hair disappearing into the slacks he's unbuttoning.

Yummy.

"You hungry?" Seb asks me and I quickly swipe at my mouth to make sure I'm not dribbling.

"She looks it." Ford grins.

"There're some cans in the cupboard," Seb says. "Zac, can you warm something up?"

Oh God. I can't breathe right. It's labored and rough. Do they hear it too?

"What are we going to do about clothes?" I ask again, all too aware that I'm without panties and wearing a skirt.

"We can get some things in a few days," Seb assures me.

A few days are too many. I need new underwear. Now.

Leo disappears with Sebastian in the bedroom and closes the door, ignoring my utter mortification of Sebastian's parting words.

They're serious. A few days. This is going to be torture.

8

Zac Stone—Electronic Security Agent

How can someone look ridiculous and fucking cute at the same time?

Wearing my oversized shirt and Ford's boxer briefs folded a few times to keep them from falling down, Clove moves her knight to take out my queen. She jumps with a victorious squeal and I watch as her tits bounce with the movement.

Fuck. Being cooped up in here with her for four days has been a test for us all. Clove has grown irresistible over the last few years. She's evolved into this woman who lures you in with her innocent personality and nearly kills you with those fucking curves of hers. A wet fucking dream for all of us. We'd all be lying if we said we haven't thought about fucking her, enlightening her to what her body is capable of. I know I certainly have. And Seb, with a few beers in him, is all too quick to tell me every vivid detail of what he'd love to do to her.

"He lets you win," Ford snorts.

Seb rolls his eyes and paces the perimeter of the small space.

"You got ants in your pants?" I growl to him.

"You don't let me win, do you?" Clove asks, her jaw open and brown eyes wide.

"No, brat," I say with a devilish wink. Of course I let her win. I get off from the elation on her sweet fucking lips.

"We should go to the grocery store today," Seb says. "It's almost two hours from here, so we'll probably get back late. And then I can get online and check my emails. I put out the feelers before we left, so we should have some answers by now."

Ford gets to his feet and stretches. "I'm down for that. I can't eat another can of baked beans if my life depended on it."

Clove practically runs to the bedroom and comes back a minute later wearing her skirt and shoes. "Let's go." She beams.

"When the sun sets," Sebastian stalls, making her deflate.

"It's only another hour," I say to soften the sad look on her face. "Come on. I'll try and beat you this time."

9

Leo King—Open Source Intelligence Agent

We stop for a piss break somewhere around three in the morning. Seb says we're about an hour away from being back at the small hunting cabin. We spent more time at the store than we planned with Seb having emails informing us that William was clean and that Ren character was spotted on CCTV elsewhere at the time of the attempted hit and run. As much as we wanted to make either of them responsible for being behind this, neither of them checked out. Unfortunately. I'd love nothing more than to put my fist through William's prissy boy face. The plates on the car were fake so not traced back to anyone. Jack has been making appearances and doing interviews on the incident, even going as far as leaving a tearful plea to leave his daughter alone. The police are involved but have no leads either. It's a stalemate. We need to keep her away until we discover who tried to ram her down. Perhaps it was just an accident, wrong place, wrong time, but the shady plates and them fleeing points to something more sinister.

My neck is killing me from being cramped in the back. I'm supposed to be watching Clove while they're outside pissing. Now would be the time to switch up the seating arrangement. Ford or Sebastian can climb their big asses in the back. I'm done.

I unbuckle and maneuver to the middle bench seat where Clove sleeps. She trembles and it's enough to have me removing her seat belt and pulling her slight frame into my lap. Once her head is resting on my chest, I drag the belt over us and snap it in. We've all been overstepping these last few days. Things are tense, or intense is a better word for it. Clove is like a ticking time bomb with her subtle looks. The way she squeezes her thighs together whenever she's watching one of us shows how fucking ripe and horny she is. Pure little Clove has a hunger inside her that no punk like William Warner could satisfy.

I rub my big hands on every inch of her in an attempt to warm her back up. She moans in appreciation, burrowing her face against my jacket. Once she seems more relaxed and is no longer shaking, I settle. My gaze drifts to the front of the tree line where Ford stands watching the road while Seb and Zac are locked in conversation.

With her hair right under my nose, I quickly grow intoxicated by her scent. The urge to touch her everywhere is intense. It's always so fucking difficult to stay away from Clove Sterling. Hard as hell to remain professional when all I want to do is rip her clothes off with my teeth and fuck her senseless.

Possessiveness washes over me. I know I'm not the only one who salivates over our sweet girl. Seb practically growls like a goddamn caveman when she's near. Ford blatantly checks out her tits and ass, all the while shamelessly flirting with her. And Zac, despite acting like he's the professional of the bunch, eyefucks her so hard I nearly get pregnant just from watching.

It's a problem.

Four men, hard as fuck all the time over one woman.

A woman none of us can have.

Fuck, being responsible sucks sometimes.

I can tell the moment she wakes because her breathing is slightly off. I wait for her to slide out of my lap or speak, but she remains still. My greedy hands rub her as though she's still cold, lingering on her ass. Without thought, I kiss the top of her head.

Fuck.

The side door opens and I jerk my head to meet the agitated glare of Ford. I shoot him a *You snooze, you fucking lose* smirk that has him hopping in the front seat. Zac joins him up front, leaving me to deal with Seb.

"That's not safe," he hisses.

"She's always safe with me," I grind out.

Again, I wait for her to move, but she pretends to sleep. *Good girl. I'll keep you safe and warm.*

"We're killing time," I mutter and nod at the back.

Seb glowers at me before he climbs in behind us. The back lights up as he looks shit up on his phone. Zac and Ford carry on a low conversation as we take off. My heart thunders in its cage at being allowed this stolen moment with her.

And she's awake.

I rub the outside of her thigh softly over her skirt. When I reach the hem and my fingertips dance over her bare flesh, she quivers. This time, it's not the cold making her body tremble. It's my touch. I'm all man and I know what a woman likes and needs. I skim my fingers along her bare thigh all the way to her knee before running them up again. Her breath hitches when I flatten my palm and push it beneath her skirt.

Slow down, Leo. You're going to get your ass kicked.

I start to pull my hand away, but her small hand gently grips my wrist as though to say, *Don't stop.*

Her grip tightens as she guides my palm back up her thigh. That's all the permission I need. I caress her flesh and try to tame my own breathing while also trying to ignore the way my dick is hard as fucking stone against her. There's no doubt she feels every inch of the granite I'm packing. My fingers slide all the way up until I feel the edge of her panties. She gasps lowly, only loud enough for me to hear, and her legs widen to allow me access. Fuck. This is so wrong on so many levels, but I can't stop myself. Her pussy is right there for the taking. She wants me to take it.

I need to retreat. To back the fuck away. To not do what I want to do.

Yet, I can't.

I move my hand and run my knuckle along her panties. I become fixated on the small wet spot. The more I rub against it, the wetter it gets. Her breathing is heavy, but she's stifling her sounds, as though she doesn't want to get caught either.

Partners in crime.

I can live with that.

Kissing her on top of the head, I let her know I'm with her 100 percent. My fingers continue to rub her more firmly, fixating on the nub beneath the fabric that seems to pulse with need. If we were alone, I would rip her panties off and suck on her greedy clit until she screamed my name like a motherfucking prayer.

A gasp.

Loud enough that I wonder if anyone heard it.

Seb's phone rings and he starts talking in hushed tones to one of the guys from Advanced Security. I take the opportunity while he's distracted and the guys up front are talking.

"Open up more, sweetness," I whisper, urging her thighs to move wider apart.

She lets it fall to the side, opening up to me. Her panties are soaked. I push them aside and tease her dripping slit with the tip of my finger. When I ease it into her tight hole, she suppresses a whine that I mostly feel rather than hear.

Fuck.

Fuck.

I'm fingering Clove, our client.

Nah, fuck that.

She's always been more than just that and I don't want to stop. I can't stop. The guys would have to kill me before I'd let go of her willingly at this point. Slowly, I fuck her with my finger while rubbing at her clit with my thumb. She's doing a damn fine job of keeping still despite all the small twitches and breathing hitches indicating her enjoyment. I can tell the moment she comes because her body clenches tightly around my finger and she sucks in a loud breath of air. Her body trembles and I feel fucking satisfied as hell to have just gotten her off. If these bastards weren't in here, I'd have her panties off and riding my dick.

But we're not alone.

Goddammit.

"How is she?" Ford asks from up front.

I wiggle my finger inside of her, loving the way she gasps. "Perfect."

"Are we nearly home?" she croaks out, feigning having just woken up. "I'm hungry."

"I'm hungry too," I mutter, my voice husky and dripping with insinuation.

Sliding my finger out, I allow her panties to slide into place and I leave a trail of wetness along her inner thigh. I bring my finger to my nose and inhale her sweet scent. She lifts her head to look up at me. In the dark, her brown eyes flare with wild lust. Slipping the finger into my mouth, I suck her honey off my finger and love the way she licks her lips as if she's just as hungry.

"About fifty more miles," Zac assures us. "Relax and try to sleep."

I sure as fuck won't be sleeping. Not with this hard-on trying to rip through my slacks.

10

Clove Sterling—The Client

Holy shit.

Holy shit.

Leo just fingerfucked me and I came so hard I saw stars. Oh my God. This is bad, I think. It has to mean I'm some horrible person if I'd let one of my guys do me dirty with my three other guys in such close proximity.

And yet, I think part of the allure was the fact they were so close. That at any time someone could look over and catch us. *I want them to see me.* It's always been my fantasy.

Leo's hand settles back on my thigh and lust douses me with his touch once more at the memory of me falling outside the outhouse and them all standing over me. I'm perverted. But I don't think I care. If something can feel that good, it can't be wrong, right? I want to straddle him and grind against his cock. I want to press my lips to his and kiss him until I'm out of breath.

Jesus, I'm pathetic.

William really did a number on me.

Am I this desperate?

Leo doesn't seem disturbed or disgusted. In fact, he

seems rather pleased. I press my lips to his neck near his ear and whisper, "Thank you."

He squeezes my thigh hard. "You're welcome."

⟡

Crunch.

My heart rate slams against my ribcage as I wake up, afraid. My hands grip the sheet beneath me and I stare at the expanding darkness of the small room.

Crunch.

I can hear a stick breaking beyond the thin walls and Seb speaking in growly tones. I then recognize Leo's voice. Zac's soft snores can be heard nearby on the sofa. But apart from that, it's all too quiet. The temperature has dropped even more since I fell asleep in the Tahoe on the drive back. I don't even remember getting back here.

Cold and quiet.

Man, I miss my room and my house.

And my dad.

Tears threaten, but I blink them back. I'm a grown woman, for Christ's sake. A solid body beside me burns with heat, warming me up. Ford. I sigh, feeling less afraid. Ford, always intuitive, runs his strong fingers through my hair.

"You okay?"

"Cold," I whimper. I'm cold and upset.

His palm runs down my spine and settles on my ass, like we're lovers lying in our bed, not client and guard. I open my mouth to tell him this feels too good, that it's confusing me and making me want more, but before I can speak, he hauls me across his thighs. "Come here," he grunts. "Much warmer this way."

He's lost his suit jacket and dress shirt since we've been here and opts for sweatpants and just a thin T-shirt to sleep in. Unlike me, he had a change of clothes in the Tahoe. I finally picked up some clothes tonight from the store. The thin fabric of the nighty I bought is the only thing that separates us. I cling to his chest with my cheek resting against his collarbone, enjoying the way his heat burrows through me. His palms rub up and down my thighs, reminding me of hours ago in the car with Leo.

Oh, God.

"Ford," I whisper. "I did something bad."

"Yeah? What's that?" His voice is husky and strained.

"I, uh, I let…" I trail off.

"What did you do, babe?"

I tilt my head up and whisper against the side of his throat. "I let Leo touch me."

I'm flipped onto my back so quickly, I nearly cry out. Ford settles his lean, strong body over mine, pinning me to the lumpy mattress. His cock is hard and presses shamelessly against my center, forcing my legs to part for his hips to settle against me in the most torturous yet perfect way.

His nose touches mine and his breath is hot against my mouth. "You did fucking what?"

"It just happened. In the car," I breathe. I'm embarrassed, but I don't regret it. It felt good. Really good. And now, I'm turned on just thinking about it. Especially by the way he rubs against me.

"How did he touch you?"

My breathing increases with the thoughts. "With his fingers."

"Where?" he growls.

"Between my legs."

"Where?" he demands again.

"My pussy."

"He did it with us right there?" he asks in astonishment. He sounds equal parts impressed and pissed as hell.

"I'm sorry," I mutter. "It was wrong. There's something wrong with me." My brows furrow as I allow my own words to wash over me. Why do I want them all? I'm greedy and slutty. But if I'm being honest with myself, I don't care that it's slutty. I care about them all and always have. Why is that wrong?

His lips press to mine softly. "There is nothing wrong with you." He grinds his cock against me and my entire body shudders with delight. "Everything is right with you, Clove."

I grip his strong biceps and dig my heels into his ass. Hot breath. Strong body. Manly scent. In the dark, I want to be consumed by him.

"I don't know what has come over me," I murmur. "I'm practically on fire with need. It's embarrassing." I'm near tears at how much of a whore this makes me. Letting one of my guys finger me, and then hours later another one dry hump me.

"You do not have to be embarrassed," he assures me in a whisper. "Let me help this time, babe."

I relax at his words. He doesn't seem horrified at the way I clutch desperately onto him. In fact, like Leo, he seems into it. His hips flex and I bite on my lip to keep from crying out. When his large palm grips my tit over my gown, a moan slips out. I crave more of his touch and I clumsily pull it down, baring myself to give him more access. As soon as I have it pulled down, his hot palm touches my skin, causing a ripple of consuming need to zing through me. He caresses me gently at first, and then his hand becomes desperate and firm, squeezing and teasing, pinching the nipple that has pebbled for him.

"Fuck," he growls. "Look how perfect you are."

I melt under his intense praise. Leaning down, he takes my lips in a hard, rough kiss before slowly trailing his way down to my chest. When his soft lips brush against my nipple, I arch my back up. His tongue flicks out, and he laves it against the peaked flesh. He sucks the nipple into his mouth and the room glitters with color.

Holy shit.

His other hand slides down between my thighs and he rubs my pussy over my panties. I get lost on the sick pleasure of the idea Leo was there only hours ago. My internal voice screaming, *"Fuck me, Ford. Fuck me like the bad girl I am."*

Shit, I'm a mess. My pussy throbs as pleasure pulses there, sending my eyes rolling into the back of my head and my toes curling. I come hard with images of both Leo and Ford doing filthy things to me at the same time. I'm desperate to throw Ford to his back and just take what I need. A little growl rumbles in my chest, making him grin. The wicked gleam in his eyes says he knows exactly where my thoughts are.

I've barely come down when we hear footsteps enter the cabin. Ford slides off me quickly like I'm a fire he's too close to. We're both breathing heavily. I want to talk to him about it, but we've been interrupted.

"Good," Seb grunts. "You're awake. I'm tired as hell."

I remain lying on my back, my heart thundering in my chest. Ford curses but climbs out of the bed. They exchange some words and Ford hisses for Zac to wake up as well. Zac grumbles for Seb to "fuck off" and doesn't make any moves to leave from the couch. Seb's shoes get kicked off and his gun makes a thunking sound as he sets it on a nearby table. Then comes his shirt and slacks before he's sliding into bed with me.

I'm going to combust. No sane person could survive these men. You'd have to be a saint not to want them. I'm no saint.

My mind is back on when he was looking up at me from the yard of my house the day we had to leave without a trace. The way he stared up at my nearly naked body. How he picked up my vibrator. The way his blue eyes blaze whenever I'm near.

Being cramped in this tiny cabin with four beastly gods is bad. So bad. I'm horny and vulnerable. Between my breakup and then nearly getting mowed down, my emotions are in turmoil. And I want them to make it all go away. To make it all better, giving me what I've been missing out on all this time. *Save me, Seb.*

"Clo?" His voice is raspy and deep.

"Yes?"

"We need to talk."

Fuck, he knows.

11

Sebastian Constantine—Chief Protection Specialist

Those bastards must think I'm stupid. I could hear her panting. Whimpering like a little kitten being stroked. Damn, as I lie here, I can fucking smell her arousal. She's burning up with fucking need and I want so badly to taste her.

"Don't blame them," she blurts out.

I tense. *Them?* "Blame who?"

"Erm." She shifts so she's facing me. "I left my things at home, so I don't have what I need to sate this craving inside me." The plea for me to understand radiates from her.

She's talking about her vibrator. The pink little toy that was wet with her juices when I caught her in the act nearly a week ago. She got off on me seeing her. I sit up and push the covers from the bed.

I'll be damned if I don't help her with her needs. The other guys sure as hell don't have a problem helping out.

"Show me, Clo," I rumble. "Show me where you crave to be touched."

Sprinklings of goose bumps rise over her exposed skin. The barely-there nightie she bought sits around her waist. Her cotton panties are damp down the center. Her hand slides down between her legs and she breathes, "Here."

"Take your panties off and show me where you touch yourself," I growl. We've crossed so many lines and I'm the worst of all because I'm in charge and trusted to look after her by her father.

But fuck if I haven't wanted her for so long. I crave to have her delicate hands on me and my own rough ones caressing her forbidden fruit.

She slips her hand into her panties and sighs. I need to see more and she needs me too. She gets off on being seen and watched. I slowly skim my palms up her legs and grip her panties before tearing them and throwing the scraps to the floor. I nudge her foot and she complies with my silent command. *Open up for me.* My heart is pounding inside my chest and my dick is straining in my boxers as she drops her knees and opens up to me like the clouds parting in a storm to show a sliver of heaven. Pink wet flesh tucked between smooth folds.

"You shave?" I gulp.

"Wax. I don't like the hair against my fingers," she moans. She's shaking. Her entire form is vibrating, the ripe hole twitching with hunger to be filled. I want so badly to lean forward and taste her.

"Touch yourself, Clo," I croak through a dry throat.

Just as she arches her back and torments her clit, Zac sits up on the sofa where he'd been sleeping, or at least pretending to. He doesn't say anything and neither do I. This has been brewing for years and if I didn't think she was ready for it to happen I'd smack the shit out of all of us. But we all fucking want it and we're hitting the peak of dancing around the subject. This was always going to happen. It wasn't a matter of if, just when.

I need to see all of her. I reach forward and grab the hem of her nighty, tearing the fabric from her body, exposing her taut stomach and perky tits. Her rosy nipples pebble as her chest heaves and her moans filter through the room.

"Taste her," Zac tells me, his tone rough and filled with lust.

Fuck.

No turning back now. Not that I fucking want to. My morals drained from me somewhere around the place we pissed. Out here, morals don't exist.

I palm her tits and squeeze them, my thumbs strumming the tight nipples, and then I can't wait any longer. "Move your hand, Clo," I growl. "Let me feast on you, baby."

A rumble escapes me as I dive in and devour her. Sucking on her clit gets me a loud groan from her and her ass lifts to assist in rubbing her pussy against my face. Fucking sweet like honey. I lick and taste, swirling my tongue around her clit. I release one of her tits and bring my fingers to her tight hole, slipping two straight inside her and relishing the feeling of finally being inside her.

She won't need that pink piece of rubber ever again. Not with me around.

I pump my fingers, sucking and tormenting her clit until her legs crash closed against my head and her body tenses all over. I don't retreat. I push her limits and continue to force another orgasm from her body. I feel a hot splatter on my arm and lift my head to discover Zac rubbing his cock, his climax spurting over Clo's chest and face.

I use his manmade lube to rub her hard nipple, pinching until she calls out in pain. Then, I release it and Zac leans down to suck away the sting.

"That was beautiful," he growls against her flesh.

"We've got company, boys!" Ford bellows from beyond the bedroom. "Fuck!"

Zac and I, despite seconds away from taking this thing with Clo even further, scramble into action. I'm dressed with my Glock in hand within seconds.

"Eyes on her," I order as I creep out of the cabin with my weapon drawn.

I can hear Clo whispering to Zac beyond the thin cabin walls, but he shushes her. Quietly and with my eyes squinting against the dark night, I look for my boys. I see a glint of metal in the moonlight and Leo nods ahead of him to the Tahoe.

Scraaaape.

Crunch.

Crack.

Someone is hiding behind the vehicle and not being very quiet about it. A glimpse of movement to my left has me swinging my weapon in that direction. But when I lock eyes with Ford as he stealthily moves forward, I move my weapon back toward the sound. The three of us circle around the vehicle.

As soon as I peer around the back of the Tahoe, I let out a curse. A decent sized bear is trying to get inside the vehicle after some food that's been locked away.

"Bear!" I call out and raise my Glock in the air. It's risky to make noise, but I'm not shooting the fucker. He's just hungry.

Pop!

The bear lets out a frightened snarl and takes off running into the woods away from us. Ford comes up behind me and laughs.

He sniffs the air and then gives my shoulder a squeeze. "Looks like the bear wasn't the only asshole hungry."

Of course this fucker would be able to smell pussy from a mile away.

"Yeah, yeah," I grumble. "This cabin is a little too close-quartered for my liking. We need to research a better location."

"Someplace with a fucking shower," Leo agrees as he approaches. These sponge baths are getting damn old. This asshole sniffs the air too. "Not that I'm complaining about *that* smell." He smirks, looking extra devilish in the moonlight.

We definitely have to get out of here. And soon.

12

Leo King—Open Source Intelligence Agent

I stare at the newspaper I bought and shake my head. Last night Seb toyed with the idea of leaving this cabin hell-hole and I can't agree more. Especially now that I'm having doubts about the people after Clove and Jack.

"Is that Jack?" Seb asks from behind me.

He snatches the paper and his blue eyes skim over the words. His features, which had been amused turn furious. "What the hell is he doing?"

"Not hiding and staying out of the limelight, that much is clear," I grunt.

Clove giggles from the other room and I can hear Ford teasing her. I love when she laughs. Makes everything not feel so rigid and stressful. She breathes fresh air into our world, that's for damn sure.

"He's giving exclusive interviews about how hard it was after Marlene's death. About how difficult it was raising Clo. He's playing the public. What the hell?" Sebastian growls.

"Certainly not acting like someone who thinks his family's life is in danger," I grumble.

Seb slams the paper down on the table and runs his fingers through his hair. It's seen better days. This cabin is getting the best of all of us. We're going stir crazy and despite our sponge baths, we smell ripe as fuck. He paces the small space and then stops, folding his arms across his chest.

"There's no fucking breadcrumbs leading us anywhere. I've had all of our best resources pulled and they all say the same thing."

"Which is?" I ask, my tone low and murderous. "No one had motive and the leads all head home."

Acid pours into my joints, solidifying my muscles and grinding my bones.

"Home as in…Jack?" I shake my head. No way. Her father wouldn't…

"It's a stunt." His jaw clenches and fire blazes in his eyes. "He played us—his own daughter—in order to further his political agenda."

I rise and grab his shoulders, hoping to calm my friend. "You can't be sure."

He looks away. "No, but I know. He's reenacting what happened with his wife. Sympathy. Look at all of these." He picks up paper after paper, magazine covers with Jack plastered all over them.

"And if you're wrong?" I have to ask, but the clenching of my gut tells me he's not.

"My duty to protect her will never wane," he assures me, his eyes pinning me in place. "But the plan has changed. I want us packed up within the hour. We're headed up north."

I lift a brow at him. "What's up north?"

"Indoor plumbing. Electricity. My bed."

"Your place?" I ask, shock lacing my tone. "I didn't even know you still owned that house. You're never there."

Guilt flashes in his eyes. "I still own it."

"Out with it, Seb."

He scrubs at his face. "Rachel lives there."

Rachel lives there.

Rachel, his ex-fiancée, who cheated on him while he was away just before we took the Sterling detail?

He sighs, placing his hands on his hips. "I should have told you," he admits in defeat.

"It's been six fucking years, Seb," I snarl. "Why the fuck is she still there?"

"It's complicated."

"Going to need more than that."

Scratching the back of his head, he scrunches up his features. "I was thinking about retiring."

"Retiring?" I scoff. "You're what? Forty?"

"Thirty-six," he grumbles, giving me the middle finger. He knows I know how old he is. We've been friends for over a decade. He's the only reason I came into this job after a tour overseas. He pulled me off a ledge when my death count began to haunt me in my sleep and the only way to shut the ghosts out was with a bottle of Jack and a fistful of sleeping pills. Seb taught me to put my skill set to use. Help people who needed protecting.

"Awfully young to throw in the towel and what? You're going to go back to Rachel? She fucking cheated on your ass." I sound pissed because I am.

"Fuck no. Rachel has nothing to do with it. I let her stay at my place because she was knocked up."

His words nearly knock the breath from my lungs.

"Yours?" I wheeze.

He shakes his head. "No."

Fuck.

"Mine?" I ask, terrified of the answer. My head swims with the memories of all the times we shared her in the bedroom. I always used a condom. *Didn't I?*

"No, asshole," he grumbles. "You think I'd keep that shit from you?"

No. But it would appear he does keep fucking secrets.

"The prick she…" He trails off and his jaw clenches. "The prick she fucked while I was working." The blacks of his pupils swallow the color, making him appear beastly.

"You soft cunt," I bark out, my tone mocking. "You let her live in your place with the kid of some town rat she was banging. Does he live there too?"

Folding my arms over my chest, I glare at him. Rachel was a bitch who did a number on him. She was insatiable and that's when he brought me into their bedroom, but it didn't matter how much he fucked her or how many men he brought into their bed, she was always going to cheat. She was a manipulative bitch who couldn't get over her ex, Joey. She was using Seb at first, to make her then ex Joey jealous, but Seb had blinders on when it came to her. He couldn't see that she was using him. Took him finding Clove to finally forget Rachel existed. Clove was like a breath of fresh air, an angel sent to us to heal our broken fucking souls, shattered black hearts.

"Casey Roberts." Seb smirks.

"What?"

"Rachel's ex and baby fucking daddy. He ran off with Casey Roberts."

No way.

"Fat Casey?" I scoff. She wasn't just fat, she had a bug eye and put her ass all over town to whoever would ride it.

Seb is chuckling now, holding his gut from the effort. It's a sight rarely seen on him and causes a contagious reaction in me. Tears stream from my eyes and our laughter echoes in the open space.

When I get myself under control, the atmosphere thickens as we both grow serious again. "So why retirement?"

Furling his brows, he looks at the ground, kicking at the dirt. "I just…Clo was going to marry that fucker one day and I didn't want to stick around for it. I couldn't stand to see her married to a jumped-up prick. Could you? Being around her knowing she would never be ours?" He looks toward the cabin.

"She will always be ours, brother," I tell him, because it's true.

"And Jack…" he trails off. "I was just tired of wanting, watching, waiting. One day I'd like to settle the fuck down. Get married maybe. Have a kid. Enjoy my life rather than protecting someone else's. I have land, property, money. This was never supposed to be permanent for me. I would promote your ass and sit mine on a couch."

My eyes widen at his candid words. "When were you going to tell me?"

He flashes me an apologetic look. "It wasn't decided yet, Leo. Get your panties out of a wad and let the others know we're going to roll out." Subject officially closed according to Seb.

"Right, boss," I concede as I push past him. "But we're not done. As soon as I get a proper shower and a hot meal in my stomach, we're going to talk about this."

"Yeah, fine," he grunts.

Sit his ass on a couch? Yeah fucking right. Seb can't sit still. He'll drive himself insane without us there to piss him off. He needs us and we need him. He's the cement in our very stable wall. Without him, we tumble.

I walk into the other room to find Clove sitting on the couch between Ford and Zac. Her head is resting in Ford's lap where he strokes his fingers through her hair while Zac rubs her feet. It makes me want to pluck her up and toss hers over my shoulder. To carry her far away from them, so I can keep her to myself for a little while. I can do unspeakable things to her before I have to share her with the rest.

"You're growling," she says, grinning. God, even roughing it out in the middle of nowhere, she is beautiful. The guys are all dirty and unshaven and starting to stink, but Clove is supple and pretty and completely kissable.

"Can we talk?" I ask her. "Alone."

She takes note of my seriousness and jumps up, a frown marring her features. Her hand grabs onto mine and she guides me over to the bed. Zac and Ford grumble, but leave us be, shutting the door behind them. I pinch the bridge of my nose when we're alone.

"Your dad is splashed all over the news. Doing interviews and shit," I utter. I've always been a straight shooter.

"What? He's supposed to be lying low." She bites on her pink bottom lip and shifts nervously on her feet.

"Well, he's not." I run my fingers through my hair and pin her with a hard stare. "It's possible that this was all a ploy."

"For publicity?" she scoffs. "You think someone tried to have me killed to get him to do interviews?"

"Not killed. Just appear to be targeted, Clove."

Her eyes widen as she shakes her head vehemently. "No. Who would that benefit?"

Girls will always believe the best in their daddies. But she didn't read the articles. I did. I saw right through that shit as did Seb. She's pacing now, swiping panicked hands through her hair.

"So, it was all fake? I'm not in danger?" she asks, tears welling in her pretty brown eyes. "We can just go home now?"

I grab her narrow hips and pull her to me to stop her frantic movements. "We can't be for sure and we won't jeopardize your safety for one second. Especially not on a hunch." I hug her tight and kiss her hair. "We're just going to relocate. Someplace safe but with better tools at our disposal. Like the fucking Internet."

She laughs, but it's tearful. "I could use a hot bath."

"I could use a real bed and not a lumpy-ass couch."

Her head tilts and she regards me with a sweet smile. The lines have been blurred for all five of us since we've been here. Definitely crossed. I'll be damned if I toe the line based on professionalism. Not when the most gorgeous woman I know is staring up at me with her lips parted just begging for a kiss.

I slide my palm to her throat and grip her jaw. She gasps when I pull her chin down to expose her supple mouth to me. A small moan of anticipation escapes her and I steal it. I lean down, press my lips to hers, and suck away that need. My eager girl thrusts her tongue against mine, desperate for the kiss every bit as much as me. Her palms roam up my shirt and settle at my neck. Turning her toward the wall, I back her into it. Our kiss becomes more frantic. My hands grip her ass and I lift her. She wraps her legs around my waist and we both groan in unison when my cock rubs against her center through our clothes.

"God, Clove," I murmur against her mouth. "The things I want to do to you."

"So, do them," she challenges, breathless.

I pull away and smirk at her. "I'm not the only one who wants to do them. You're poking a hornet's nest, babe. We're all about to swarm."

"You say this like it's a bad thing," she says and then bites on her bottom lip. "Four gorgeous men wanting to do dirty *things* to me. Can't see what's so bad about that."

Her teasing words only make me harder. I grind against her. "Maybe I don't like to share," I grumble. "At least Seb's old ass will be gone and out of my way. Less dicks to lure you away from me."

"You can share me." She laughs, but then her brows crash together. "Wait…Sebastian gone? What do you mean?"

Oh, shit.

"Nothing."

"Leo," she hisses. "Don't you dare nothing me. I'm not just some client anymore, I never have been, and I'm not a child. Tell me what that meant."

I let out a huff. "You're right, you were never just a client, Clove."

"Tell me," she demands.

"He wants to retire or some shit."

"Oh, hell no."

Fuck.

13

Clove Sterling—The Client

Sebastian is retiring? Since when? He's like in his thirties. And he's mine. He can't retire. Sliding to my feet, I push Leo away from me.

"Fuck," he groans. "Don't say anything."

"Screw that," I screech. "He can't leave us like that!"

Storming from the room into the sitting area, I find him discussing something with Ford and Zac. As soon as he catches my furious stare, he holds his hands up in defense. Hands that just last night roamed my body. The fucker led me on, knowing he was going to leave.

"You don't get to retire," I spit out, shoving his stone-hard chest. He goes nowhere. "You don't get to leave me."

Shame has him looking at the other guys. "Clo…" He clenches his jaw and flashes me a hard stare. "We need to pack up and leave. We'll discuss this later."

"No! We're discussing this right now!" I slap at his chest, letting all my fury and betrayal aim their way at him until he's had enough.

"Fine," he bellows. "We'll talk about it now. Outside."

I scream when he bends and tosses me over his shoulder. My fists pummel his muscled ass until I hear the other three guys sniggering. I trade my fists for shooting them the middle finger on the way out the door. As soon as we're outside, Seb stalks away from the cabin through the thicket of trees. Once we're alone, he sets me to my feet.

"Calm down," he snarls.

"No," I hiss, my heart in my throat. "I need you. You can't leave me. I don't even know who I am without you guys." I choke on my truth.

"Come here," he grumbles, pulling me to him. He holds me as I let the emotion overtake me and cry against him. I've never really thought about any of them ever leaving me. It's too unbearable to ever imagine.

"Is it Dad? Did you have a falling out about what happened? Is it me?" My heart sinks at that prospect. Was it because he saw me pleasuring myself and we crossed a line? Oh God. Him pleasuring me…

"It's not you," he says fiercely. "Well, not in the way you may think."

My body stiffens. I look up at him through my lashes, heat flooding my cheeks and sorrow gripping my heart at the thought of losing him. "What?" A chill races up my spine, the air frigid with a sense of fragility. Is this all over before we've even had a chance to explore it?

"Before we came out here…" he trails off and scowls. "I was having a hard time watching you with William. He didn't deserve you." He lifts a hand and strokes his knuckle along my cheek, swiping off a tear that dropped there without permission. "I wanted you and it was unprofessional and unethical."

He wanted me?

"But then?" I ask, hope in my voice.

"Then we crossed some lines and I don't want to go

back over them. My plans have been derailed," he admits in defeat. "Now…now you're not with that fucking idiot William. I'm left with the three men I trust more than anything all falling head over fucking heels for the girl I want. The girl I've wanted for a long ass time, Clove."

"So, share me," I say on a desperate breath. Choosing or singling one of them out to date would be impossible. Greed, lust, need, my stupid heart has me wanting them all.

"It's not competing if you share." I try to convince not just him but myself. Why can't they share me? It's no one else's business and it's what I want.

He dips down and kisses my lips, causing a glimmer of hope to inflate my chest. "I'm still figuring things out."

"We'll figure them out together," I assure him, deepening the kiss. "But you don't just get to leave me. Not after all this time. After everything we've been together. Not after you finally notice me." I groan through kisses.

He scoffs, pulling away slightly. "Finally notice you? I've been aching for you long before it was morally acceptable, baby. You've starred in one too many of my fantasies. Now my fantasies are getting more complicated."

I lift a brow. "Oh? How so?"

His gaze drifts off. "Last night, having Zac in there with us, I thought I'd need you to myself. But, it was…"

"Hotter. It was hotter having him tell us what to do and watch," I whisper, my pussy pulsing with just the memory of it.

He darts his gaze back to mine. "It was."

"I'm all for exploring your complicated fantasies," I tell him with a sly grin. "I have a few of my own."

"Oh yeah?" he challenges as he grips my hips and twists me so I'm facing a thick tree. "Hold on." It's spoken deep and commanding, sending excitement coursing through my blood. They've intoxicated me and I'm riding the high, hoping never to come down from it.

I dig my fingers into the bark and smile when I feel him working at my jeans. He shoves them down, roughly scraping the flesh of my thighs as he does. It's needy and rushed and I fucking love it. Pushing them to my ankles, he then palms my ass.

"Look at you," he growls as he squeezes my butt cheek. "So long I've thought about getting you alone like this."

My heartrate races in my chest. "What are you going to do now that you have me?"

"You know what I'm going to do. What I've been thinking about every goddamned night for years." He slides my panties down and pushes them to where my jeans sit. "I'm going to finally know what it feels like to be inside you, Clo. And once I'm there, I may never want to leave."

He fumbles with his belt behind me. Then, his hot cock is rubbing down the crack of my ass, teasing me. "Beg me to fuck you," he orders. "I need to hear it, baby."

"Fuck me," I breathe, shoving my ass against his dick. It jolts against me. "Sebastian. Stop teasing and fuck me already. I've been waiting for this too, for so long. Show me what it's supposed to be like. Fuck me hard."

His groans have a thrill shooting through me. He starts rubbing his cock between my thighs and then up along my wetness that's leaking from my body. Back and forth. Back and forth. He rubs at me but never tries to enter me. It drives me crazy. I'm making a mess on his cock with my arousal. Gripping the tree so I don't fall, I bend my body and push against the head of his cock. My pussy seems to be a magnet for his thickness. His tip teases my needy little hole.

"Fuck me like you own me, Sebastian," I hiss, almost delirious with the ache. "Make me yours at last." My breathing is rapid. The sensation of pure, undiluted need rages inside my blood stream, making me wriggle my ass to complete our connection. He doesn't make me wait any longer. His thick girth pushes into me, stretching me to the point of near pain.

"Oh God," I whisper, my legs almost buckling.

He slides a hand to my front and rubs at my clit. Mixing the pleasure with pain, a chaotic duo confusing all my thoughts and functions. The pain shouldn't feel good, but it does. It all feels too much, too good. Erotic sensations take over my body, giving me all the things I've only dreamed about. My pussy clenches around his thick cock, causing us both to moan.

"Fuck, baby, you feel so damn good. Better than I've ever imagined. I'm going to give you it all. Fuck you until you're sore."

"Make me weak, Seb. Fuck my pussy and claim me," I pant, losing all inhibitions.

His fingers dig into my hip while the other hand works me closer and closer to the edge of madness. My legs shake as euphoria takes over every part of me. "I'm coming. Oh fuck, Seb, you're making me come," I cry out.

"Yeah, Clo, fucking come all over my big dick, baby," he barks, hammering his hips into me until I feel his cock pulse and warm cum begins to fill me. Of all the times I was with my ex, it never felt like this. So all-consuming and soul stealing.

"Seb," I murmur.

Snort. Snarl. Grunt.

Pleasure is coursing through my veins when his hand leaves my hip to cover my mouth. His breath is hot against my ear.

"Shhh, baby," he whispers. "Don't make a sound."

He guides my head to turn and less than twenty-five feet away, a bear is walking past. I stiffen, swallowing back a terrified scream.

"Good girl," he utters lowly. "Good, good girl."

He continues massaging my clit as his cock re-thickens and he begins to fuck me slowly from behind still, pushing himself fully inside. He fills me all the way up with his cock, causing my entire body to reignite. I can barely breathe with his large hand covering my mouth and my pleasure stealing any air in my lungs. And it doesn't help that a ferocious bear is nearby. It seems to bring out the animal in Seb because his hips buck against me, skin slapping against skin, our barely contained moans risking our safety. At any moment, it could turn and see us. He pinches my clit and I lose it again.

A moan starts to rip from me, but his hand covers me tighter. Thick fingers covering my airways, my own hands clinging to the tree to stop myself from falling from the force of his thrusts. I'm overcome with wave after wave of release. He keeps stroking me right into oblivion. Desire explodes through me and I can't even make a sound. I feel like I'm suffocating and that somehow heightens the sensations. Fear mixed with pleasure is a combination I like more than I care to admit. My world spins in a delicious way as he lets out a ragged grunt. Then, his heat gushes into me, filling me up once more with his own climax.

So feral and claiming.

I've never been fucked like this.

It's overwhelming and amazing. Like when Ford had his way with me. And when Leo fingered me in the Tahoe. These men…they sate me. My guys have finally given me what I've always needed.

Everything.

Everything I could imagine and more.

Who knew it would take four strong, virile, manly guys to satisfy one sexually starved woman?

His hand slides from my face and he nuzzles his nose in my hair. "It's safe. The bear is gone."

Cum runs down my thigh as his cock starts to soften.

"But you're not. You're still here," I rasp out. "And I won't let you leave me."

He kisses the top of my head. "I'm not going anywhere, baby."

14

Zac Stone—Electronic Security Agent

"Warm, tight, fucking delicious. Just like I knew she would be," Sebastian says, scrubbing his hands down his face for the third time. "I can't stop thinking about her."

"You need to try and stop describing shit to me because now it's all I can think about," I grumble back at him, my hands gripping the steering wheel tight. My eyes flicker in the rearview mirror to see Clove sleeping in Ford's arms. I did everything I could not to allow myself to cross boundaries with her. I made sure whenever there was a choice to accompany her or Jack, I always volunteered to be with Jack. Because I knew one day being with her would lead us here. She was born to be ours. I knew it the first day her broken soul slipped into that limo with us. This, right now—us loving her and being with her—was inevitable.

I enjoy watching and whispering instructions, but the more he talks about how Clove felt, it has me craving a taste.

"Did your guy get any information on Jack?" he asks instead, changing the subject.

Her father, a man I respected and liked, turned out to be just another asshole willing to do anything to climb the political ladder. Including risking the life of his own fucking kid.

"His numbers were dropping in the polls," I grunt. "He needed something big."

"And money?" His tone drops, low and heavy.

"A hundred and fifty thousand moved to an offshore account. No name to trace."

"So, it *is* him," he utters in disbelief. "He did this as a stunt for publicity. I just never saw this coming. I still can't even believe it. Jack is motivated by his career, but he loves Clove."

Sometimes love takes a backseat when you're riding to the top.

Jack is a prime example of that.

She could have been killed, and the risk was worth it to her father. Motherfucker.

"So, what's the plan now?" I ask. My fists clench and my trigger finger is getting twitchy.

Seb blows out a frustrated breath. "We take a fucking shower. Get some real food in our stomachs and a decent night's sleep. Then, we deliberate because whatever happens, Clove should get a say in it, but not until we're a thousand percent sure about Jack."

Agreed.

"We need to be thorough. Recheck the background of everyone within his campaign to see if he's getting his contacts through one of them. We also need to track down the driver and hear it from his mouth. Now that we know she's not in real danger, we can reach out further to other resources to help track down this guy. He's a hired gun, so someone will have information. Time to call in favors."

Gravel crunches under the wheels of the Tahoe as I turn into Seb's long ass driveway.

"Does Leo know who lives here?" I query with an amused grin. "What about Ford?"

Seb's shoulders tense and his lips draw into a thin line. "Yeah, they know now," is all he says, grabbing the door handle and popping it open before I've even rolled to a stop.

"Speak of the devil," I snort.

Rachel Raddle stands in the glow of the porch light. Her blond hair neatly straightened and pulled over her shoulder. A full face of makeup. Tight as sin jeans and a shirt tied in a knot just below her tits, that have been pushed together by a bright pink lace bra that's showing from her having the shirt unbuttoned too far. She's trying too hard and it's comical. I study her because I'm a people watcher. I always take in every detail of everyone and everything. It's part of my job but also because I know this bitch first-hand. She fucked Seb over and therefore fucked us all over because we're a family. He gave her everything. Brought Leo and then me into their bedroom to keep her needs sated, but as soon as we were out of town working, she was whoring her ass out. When she came to him pregnant with another man's kid, I offered to kill her and the low life who knocked her up, but Seb has always been soft on her and a sucker for damsels in distress. He bought a small trailer for her and plopped it on his land. Even offered her a fucking job to take care of his property while he was away working. A good deal for her, but she confused the kind gesture and thinks she still has a chance whenever he takes time off and visits home. I figured Ford would know about Seb's dirty little secret, but I'm glad Leo knows now too that Seb let her stay even though she was a cheating skank.

My eyes dart to Clove again and I smirk. Seb's never looked at Rachel the way he looks at Clove. This shit is going to be interesting.

I climb out and look past Rachel at Seb's stately home in the middle of a clearing. Thick trees surround the perimeter. It's been ages since we've last visited.

"Hey, Zac," Rachel greets, demanding my attention. "It's been years, sugar. How've you been?"

I give her a nod of my head in greeting. "Busy."

"Still such a talker, I see," she deadpans.

"It's late," Sebastian grunts when he walks over to us. "Thanks for stocking the pantry and fridge for me."

"You pay me to do it," she says breathily. "I could hang around and help get you boys settled." Her flirty smile falls when her eyes dart behind us. The car door slams and based on the way Rachel's lip curls up and her nostrils flare, I would guess she's noticed our new addition. "And who's this?" Rachel asks, sweet and fake as fuck.

Clove prances forward between Seb and me, offering her hand to Rachel. "Clove Sterling. These are my guys..."

Rachel's brow hikes. "Your guys?"

"They're my security detail," Clove amends, shame in her voice.

I glance at Seb to find him frowning. Ford breaks up the tense moment when he saunters over to us.

"Don't know about you all, but I'm fucking tired. Chit chat all you want while I find the nearest bed." He smirks at me when he takes Clove's hand. "Come on, Lucky. Let's get you tucked in."

They walk into the barely used home with Leo trailing behind. I'm left with clingy Rachel, who's melted away some of her anger to give Sebastian one of her signature desperate smiles.

"If it's too full, you could always crash at my trailer," she purrs, running her palm down his chest.

He grips her wrist, stopping her from reaching his belt. "Not happening, Rach."

"Fine. Rest up. You'll need it because tomorrow I'm taking you guys out," she chirps. "It'll be fun. We can get wasted like old times…" She flashes me a wicked smile. "And then see where things go after that."

"Maybe," I supply, knowing full well I'm not tapping that ass ever again.

She purses her lips and lingers. Then, she reaches out to grab Seb's bicep. "Joey's been doing the hard drugs again. He and Casey broke up. He's…" She looks down at the grass. "He's been coming over high trying to get in."

I watch Seb to see if he falls for her tactics.

His jaw clenches and he looks over at his house, indecision warring in his eyes. With a heavy sigh, I offer to do the job I know he clearly doesn't want.

"I'll ride with her in her golf cart back to the trailer and check things out. Make sure she gets there safely. How about you get a shower, man? You fucking stink," I grumble, irritated that I have to babysit this bimbo.

Relief flickers in his eyes. "Thanks, man."

And then he's gone.

I'm left alone with Rachel fucking Raddle.

"Let's go," I grumble. "I'm tired as hell."

She stomps off toward the golf cart, shaking her ass like it has the power to draw me in. The only ass I crave is the one I'm being denied at the moment. Clove's perfect little ass. When Rachel sits in the driver's seat, I let out a sharp whistle and shake my head. She grumbles and scoots over. I slide into the driver's seat and start the engine. Rachel pouts as we drive the ten minutes or so through a path in the woods to her trailer. Her dogs start barking from behind her fence when they see us pull up. I shut the golf cart off and do a perimeter check. Once I deem it safe, I walk inside and make sure the doors and windows are locked. Before I can exit, she blocks my way.

"You know," she purrs, "his house is full. You could stay here with me. My bed is warm." She grips my dick through my jeans. "You still have a thing for having your dick sucked?"

As much as I do want my dick sucked, it just isn't by her.

I pat her head. "Go to bed, Rachel."

And then I leave her to growl pissed off words under her breath.

Not tonight. Hell, not ever again.

15

Clove Sterling—The Client

Sebastian's house is nice. It's too large for just him. *Who was that woman?* Three bedrooms, two bathrooms. You can tell a man decorated it. *Not a woman.* The furniture is masculine and functional. There aren't any personal photos or anything that suggests he owns this house. *Or has a mysterious woman he's never mentioned before.*

"Kitchen. Living room. Laundry room is that way," Ford says, pointing out rooms as he drags me along. "Guest rooms here and there. We'll take the master."

I follow him into the master bedroom. A large bed sits in the middle of the room across from a large, picturesque window. *Has she slept there with Seb—with any of my guys?* I walk over to the window and stare out into the dark trees.

Ford comes to stand behind me, his palms resting on my shoulders and his lips pressing a kiss to the top of my head. "You okay?"

"Yeah," I mutter. "Who was the woman?"

He tenses behind me and lets out a heavy sigh. "You don't want to know." He walks off toward the bathroom. Well, that's ominous. Now I really want to know.

I turn in time to see him shed his shirt, showing off the muscular curves of his back, and all thoughts of anything but him flee my mind. He kicks off his shoes and then pushes down his jeans, baring his ass at me. I'm left gaping when the bathroom door closes behind him. The shower starts and I'm still frozen when someone chuckles from the doorway.

Leo's brow is lifted as he regards me. "Did you see something you like?"

Heat floods my cheeks, but I refuse to let Leo make me feel bad for checking out Ford's perfect, sculpted ass. "I'm doing a comparative study," I tell him with an innocent smile. "Maybe you should take your pants off too so I can see whose is better. For research."

He peels off his T-shirt and flexes his chiseled abs. Leo is every bit the Greek god you see pictures of in books. With a last name like King and a body like his, you can't help but want to worship him from your knees. Black sparrows and flowers are artfully tattooed over the left side of his chest, making me curious to explore them closer. I wet my bottom lip with my tongue, nearly choking on a groan.

"You're really going to show me your ass?" I challenge, my heart rapidly pounding in my chest.

He shrugs his muscular shoulders. "I'm going to show you my dick too, sweetness. Give you all the evidence you need for your…research."

True to his word, he unbuckles his jeans and shoves them down. His black boxers are stretched tight over his obvious erection. Thick and hard. Holy shit.

I'm most definitely feeling the urge for a little worship…

"Come," he orders huskily.

I swallow and blink several times in shock. "W-What?"

"Well, that coming will come later. For now, let's compare."

He takes my hand and all but drags me into the bathroom where the shower is going. The glass is steamed over, so I can't see anything but Ford's blurred form.

"Hey, Ford," Leo barks out.

"Yeah, man?"

"Clove here wants to compare our dicks," Leo says like it's the most normal thing ever.

Ford laughs. "Get our girl naked and let's show her that my nine inches is preferable to your five."

"Five my ass," Leo grumbles, but his green eyes dance with amusement. "Take your clothes off, sweetness."

This is happening.

Oh my God.

My hands tremble as I fumble with my jeans. Leo reaches forward and assists. His warm fingers brushing over my stomach have a shiver rumbling through me. The shower door pushes open soundlessly.

And dear God.

Ford is an angel carved from stone. Perfect. Tanned. Sculpted muscles on his chest that I'm dying to explore more closely. But what has me transfixed is the way his bicep flexes each time he tugs at his very impressive cock. His eyes are dark with lust but still twinkle with amusement. My jeans get shoved down my thighs, causing me to exhale loudly.

"Take your shirt off, Lucky. I want to see your tits."

I bite on my bottom lip before giving in to Ford's command. Leo helps me out of my shoes and socks.

"Cute bra and panties," Leo says with a wicked grin. "They'll look cuter on the ground."

A giggle escapes me and it's infectious. Both Leo and Ford chuckle. The nerves that had been clawing their way through my bones dissipates like the steam building in the bathroom. Leo relieves me of the last of my clothes before grabbing my wrist. He tugs me into the walk-in shower. The moment I'm within reach, Ford grabs my hips and pulls me against him.

Angling my head up, I look into his heated eyes. He doesn't give me a chance to speak. Just crushes his full lips to mine in a soul-stealing kiss. His hands roam up my ribs on a trek to my breasts. When two strong hands touch my shoulders, I shiver with awareness.

Two.

I am naked with two extremely hot men.

Two men who want me as badly as I want them.

Leo pulls my hair off to one side so he can access my neck. His mouth latches onto my flesh as his palms slide to my front. A mewl crawls out of my throat when he touches my pussy. Ford smiles against my mouth, never breaking our kiss, and pinches my achingly hard nipples. Leo's dick is stone against the crack of my ass.

"Time to compare," Leo taunts, rubbing his dick against me. "We're waiting for your full report."

Ford pulls slightly away to give me a mischievous grin. "Go on, Lucky. Get a grip."

I reach between us and fist his thickness. Then, I reach behind me to grab onto Leo's cock. Both are thick and long and perfect.

"Who's the winner?" Leo rasps out, his hips gently rocking against my grip on him. *Me. I'm the winner.* He intensifies the way his fingers circle my clit until I'm trembling with need. "Hmm?"

"I, uh, I…ohhhh…" I moan.

Ford twists my nipples, making me whimper. "What's your verdict?"

"It's a tie," I whimper. "I love them both. You're both perfect."

"Good girl," Leo growls. His palms splay under my thighs and he lifts me. I can feel his dick bobbling against my pussy. My body wriggles as I seek out his cock.

"Need some help?" Ford asks with a devilish gleam in his eyes. He kneels in front of us and boldly grabs Leo's dick to help guide it into my needy body.

Leo hisses in pleasure and I let out a whine when Ford's mouth makes contact with my pussy. I'm boneless in Leo's strong arms. He easily maneuvers me up and down his length as he nips at my shoulder. My fingers find Ford's wet hair, latching on, as he sucks on my clit. I'm completely lost in this moment while these two men pleasure me. Ford's mouth is pure magic as he sucks, licks, bites me on my clit and pussy lips.

"Oh, God," I whimper. "Leo! Ford!" My orgasm steals over me, causing my core to clench. This sets Leo off because he lets out a feral grunt. His heat floods inside of me as his teeth bruise my flesh.

I've barely come down from my high before Ford is rising to his feet and greedily pulling me from Leo's grasp. The loss of Leo's dick inside of me makes me feel hollow, but seconds later, it's Ford stretching me with his cock. My legs latch around his waist while our mouths meet as he fucks me against the tile wall. He tastes like me. It sends fire burning in my stomach. I love it.

"You're fucking perfect, Lucky," Ford rumbles. He nips at my jaw before finding my ear. His hot breath tickles me there. "So fucking perfect and ours."

Ours.

Not just his.

Theirs.

Filthy images of my other two guys in the shower with us have another orgasm edging closer and closer.

"Water's getting cold," Leo murmurs from my other side. He smells like soap now and I vaguely realize he washed up while Ford's been fucking me into next week. "Besides, I'm standing in the way of someone's view."

Ford's body slaps loudly against mine, earning my undivided attention. I can feel eyes on me, but I can't look up. Ford's mouth is back on mine, demanding my complete focus. He reaches between us and gives my clit some expert massages that have me once again losing control. My head slams back against the tile with a thud. I cry out, my entire body shuddering. More heat surges inside of me.

They're filling me up.

Marking me as theirs.

Ford's dick stops twitching eventually and he slips out of me. Since the water has grown cold, he washes us both quickly. When I step out of the shower in a sex-induced haze, I find Sebastian waiting with a towel.

"Hey," I say, unable to meet his eyes as he wraps the plush towel around me.

His fingers find my chin, tilting my head up. "Hey, beautiful."

Nothing in his gaze indicates he thinks I'm dirty. If anything, lust blazes hot in his stare. I'm a little sore, but

I'm aching to have him too. He must sense my need because his nostrils flare.

I let out a squeal when he scoops me into his powerful arms. A laugh peals from me and it's then I feel some of Ford's and Leo's cum gush out of me. It's dirty but so hot too. Sebastian carries me into the master bedroom over to the bed. He sets me down before tugging the towel away.

"Let's take a look at that pussy," he growls, spreading my thighs apart. His hungry stare rakes across my sensitive area, sending shivers down my spine. "They abused it. Naughty, Clo. You're so naughty."

Ford chuckles as he saunters into the room with a towel tied at his waist. I catch Leo's stare from a chair in the corner. Having them watch as Seb lazily rubs at my pussy has my thighs clenching.

Sebastian reaches behind his neck to grab hold of his shirt. He yanks it over his head in one of those hot guy moves that melts your ovaries. I drink in his solid, tattooed chest and slight smattering of dark chest hair between his pecks. His biceps that are also covered in tattoos flex, but it's his inked, muscular shoulders I crave to lick. So much art on this man and I want to explore every part of him slowly. My eyes travel down his cut abs to his happy trail that promises more fun times inside his jeans. When he sees me peeking at him, he flashes me a smirk before undoing his jeans. The sound of flesh on flesh has me scanning the room again. Leo's kicked back in the chair with his legs stretched out in front of him and his thighs parted as he strokes his cock. He looks as though he truly is a god sitting on a throne. I'm enamored by the sight until Seb's dick teases at my opening that leaks with two other men's cum.

"All lubed up for me?" Seb asks, the thick crown of his dick breaching me. It burns slightly when he stretches me slowly, easing all the way in until he bottoms out. He leans forward to seek out my mouth. We kiss hard and sloppily as he fucks me in an aggressive yet sweet way that makes me feel safe with him. I'm too spent to come again. I just know it. But then his fingers are massaging my clit hard and fast. It almost hurts to try to wring out another orgasm. "Come for me, Clo. Don't deny me what I want."

It builds and builds until I'm crying out his name.

The world around me glitters white as I lose myself to ecstasy.

I'm dizzied with pleasure.

He groans, signaling his release, before filling me up.

"Oh God," I murmur.

I'm so sore. Everything hurts.

And yet…

"About time," Ford says to someone. "We started without you."

"No shit," Zac grunts.

Seb smiles against my lips and then pulls out abruptly. My eyes seek out Zac through heavy lids. He's naked. Gloriously naked. His lean, yet chiseled chest begs to be touched and his large cock juts out proudly in front of him. I lick my lips before meeting his hungry, almost angry stare.

I tense, panic welling up inside of me.

But then he winks.

That simple act of reassurance has me relaxing despite the way three men's cum leaks from my sore pussy.

"My turn, brat," Zac growls, his brown eyes darkening. When he first called me brat, way back when they started working for my dad, I'd taken offense. But over the years, I've come to accept it as a term of endearment.

His hands find my hips roughly and he flips me over onto my stomach. Fire cracks along my ass cheek the moment he slaps it. Before I can recover, he's pushing his overly large dick inside me.

Tears burn in my eyes as he brutally stretches me to the point of pain. He's thick and long. With every thrust, he bruises me someplace deep inside. All I can do is suppress a sob as I grip the comforter.

He slaps my ass again, making me clench around him. I whimper at the pain of it. His hand massages the sore flesh and I'm almost eager to feel the sting once more.

What's wrong with me?

He thrusts hard, hitting a spot within me that makes me jolt in surprise. His hand cracks my ass another time before gripping my hips hard. He angles me higher as he pistons his hips. The place he's found inside me throbs with each glorious stab of his monster cock.

Oh God. Oh God. Oh God.

"Oh God!" I scream when the pleasure seems to claw at me from the inside out. This orgasm is different from the others. It pulls me from this world and tosses me into another. Foreign and wonderful. I'm in unfamiliar territory.

A feral grunt tears from Zac's throat.

Then his heat floods me.

His cum fills me up, stinging my insides. I expect him to pull out, but he lays his sweaty body against my back and finds my ear. He presses a sweet kiss to the shell of my ear.

"I knew you'd be perfect, Clove," he murmurs. "So fucking perfect. And ours."

I don't have the words.

Tears of happiness and fatigue and from being overwhelmed leak from my eyes.

All I can do is nod.

Theirs.

I am theirs.

Finally.

16

Sebastian Constantine—Chief Protection Specialist

I wake to a hand flopping across my face and I groan, shoving away the man's hand. Rolling onto my side, I find Clo tucked against Leo's side. Images of last night when we all took a turn with our girl come flooding through my mind.

We're all so fucked up.

And, honestly, I can't find it in me to care.

In our case, fucked up is really hot and strangely fulfilling.

Yes, Leo is a bed hog and sleeps like a three-year-old. But he's also one of my best friends. Loyal to a fault. Would lay down his life, like he clearly demonstrated not too long ago, for the girl in his arms. And the great part is, he's not a jealous, possessive prick. None of us are. We've all dabbled a bit in polyamorous sex, but this is the first time all four of us have actively—yet in an unspoken way—pursued the same woman with more purpose than to just fuck.

All four of us deeply care for Clo.

The situation is a goddamn mess, but I'm not about to start ironing down the specifics. Last night happened, and something tells me more nights like that will happen. We'll keep little Clo here forever if we have to. That idea is enticing as hell.

I stroke my fingers through Clo's hair and inhale her sweet scent. My cock is hard against the crack of her ass. When her ass presses back against me, I realize she's awake.

"Good morning," I murmur against her hair, my arm snaking to her front. I find her clit and massage her there.

"Morning."

I kiss her shoulder and rub at her, loving the whimpers she makes. She quietly orgasms as she tries not to wake Leo. The moment she comes, I pull my finger away and suck on a few of them. Her taste is fucking addictive. Once my fingers are good and wet, I drag them along the tip of my dick to lube it up. I know she'll be dry from having gotten fucked four times in a row last night.

A tiny whine escapes her when I press the crown of my dick against her slit. Slowly, I ease into her pussy. I grip her full tit, my thumb and finger tweaking her nipple. My hips thrust against her in a steady pace that makes the bed creak.

"Clo…"

"Sebastian."

"You're the only woman for me." *I've been obsessed with you for years.*

She lets out a soft moan. "What about that girl last night?"

I do not want to talk about my ex with my dick inside Clo.

"She's not important. Watches my property while I'm gone."

"So, you and her—"

I silence her by twisting her nipple slightly until she cries out. I'll tell her about Rachel later, but now's not the time.

It doesn't take long before I'm groaning with my release. She starts giggling quietly and I sit up on my elbow to look at her.

"What's so funny?" I whisper.

She points to the way Leo's dick tents the sheet. He's still snoring, but we clearly made our way into his dream. Chuckling, I pull her away and kiss her neck.

"Come on," I growl. "Let's get you cleaned up."

⟡

Clo looks good enough to eat in one of my shirts and sweats. She has her own clothes now, but I must say I like the way she looks in mine. I throw on some track pants and a T-shirt. Leo is no longer in the bed when we come out of the bathroom. Clo loops her arm around mine as we follow the smell of bacon cooking.

So fucking glad we're home.

Amenities. Clothes. A proper kitchen.

We never have to leave.

Leo is standing in his boxers, shoving a piece of bacon in his mouth as he looks at his phone. Ford is dressed in jeans and a hoodie, a scowl on his face as he looks in the kitchen. And Zac is wearing a pair of sweats with no shirt on as he taps away on his laptop.

If they're over at the table, then who's in the—

"I made a bunch of bacon because I know how much you love it, Sebby," Rachel chirps as she comes out of the kitchen carrying a plate of bacon. She's wearing a low-cut shirt that shows too much of her boobs for breakfast time. Her skirt is too short and too revealing. I'm embarrassed for her. As soon as her eyes rake over Clo's appearance—just showered and wearing my clothes—her nostrils flare and her lip curls up. "Oh, hello," she says to Clo coolly before regarding me with one of her bright smiles. "Morning."

Clo tenses beside me. Leo grabs her wrist before pulling her to him in a hug. Rachel sets the bacon down on the table and then rushes over to me. She throws her arms around my neck and hugs me. Both Ford and Zac catch my gaze over her head, giving me a frown of disapproval.

"Morning," I grunt back, gripping Rachel's hips to pull her away.

She giggles and presses her tits against my chest. "You know how ticklish I am," she says breathily. "Don't worry. I still like it."

Clo makes a choked sound. I glower down at Rachel.

"Enough," I snap.

Rachel's eyebrow hikes up. "Sebby…"

When her hand reaches out to stroke my chest, I grip her wrist before hauling her through the kitchen and into the laundry room.

"We need to talk," I bite out as soon as I close the door behind us. I release Rachel's hand and cross my arms over my chest. "You? In my house? Cooking breakfast? Doesn't work for me, Rach. I pay you to make sure no one squats on my property while I'm gone, not to make breakfast."

"Jesus, Sebastian, you don't have to be so fucking rude." Her bottom lip trembles. Guilt floods through me.

"Sorry," I grumble. "It's just that…"

"You're fucking that girl?" She blinks rapidly at me as though she's trying to imagine it.

"It's not your business."

"The hell it ain't," she bellows. "We have history. In case you forgot."

"You're not my fiancée anymore, Rachel," I bark back. "You don't get a say in my life. You also don't get to walk into my house and do whatever the fuck you want, whenever you want. Clo is special to me. I won't have you making her feel unwelcome."

"Special?" she seethes. "Real special that she hugs the first half-naked guy at the first sign of trouble. She's probably sucking Leo's cock as we speak."

I roll my eyes at her. "Knock it off and go home. Whose cock she sucks is none of your damn business."

She storms over to me, fury blazing in her eyes. Her blond ponytail swings back and forth. I close my eyes, waiting for her impending slap. Instead, her lips press to mine.

I snap my eyes open and grab her shoulders, pushing her away. "Enough," I growl. "Go home. Tell me you didn't leave the kid alone."

"Fuck you, Sebastian." She lets out a harsh laugh. "And watch it with that girl. She's going to ruin you. Girls like her will play you all against each other. Good girls like to fuck the wild boys, but they don't settle down with them, Seb. When she's done using you, I'll be here. I always am."

I shake my head at her and push open the door. Clo stands there, fat tears in her eyes. Her eyes drift past me to Rachel. Rachel lets out a snort of satisfaction as she prances past us.

"Clo," I mutter.

"She's no one, huh?" Her bottom lip trembles. "I can handle the truth. If you really cared about me, you'd trust me with it." She turns on her heel and storms off.

"Clo, wait," I call out to her.

Her body crashes into Ford and he wraps his arms around her. His lips are pressed into a firm line. I start for them and he gives me a shake of his head before mouthing the word, "Later."

Then, they're gone.

And I'm left wondering how I fucked everything up in a matter of minutes.

17

Clove Sterling—The Client

Tequila is like gasoline on an ember.

One drop and then you have fire.

Two shots and you have a blaze.

Three shots and it spreads.

Four is an inferno.

"You're so fucking drunk, Lucky," Ford says, laughing against my neck as I grind into him. Some country song plays loud from a jukebox. It makes me want to rip off all my clothes to show him all my dance moves.

"I could use another shot," I purr, sliding my palm down his front to cup his cock through his jeans. "You think we could fuck right here and anyone would notice?"

A hot body sidles up behind me, causing me to shiver. "I'd notice, brat," Zac rumbles, running his palms up the outside of my thighs, pushing my dress up higher. "I'd notice and want a piece too."

I giggle and tilt my head back. I angle my face toward his to meet him for a kiss. Ford's lips find my neck. The tequila burns through my veins like liquid lust. I'm sure we're giving all these old people in this honky-tonk bar quite the show. All we're missing is Leo.

On cue, he shows up with another beloved shot. I break from Zac's perfectly kissable lips to accept the shot from Leo. Ford chides me against my throat, but I ignore him.

Zac twists me around so we're chest to chest. Ford grumbles that he has to take a piss.

"I'll keep her warm," Leo calls to him, his large hand grabbing my ass.

"You can't torture him forever," Zac says, his brows furling together and dark eyes penetrating me.

I curl my lip up. "I can't talk to him right now."

"Because he had a thing with psycho Rachel?" Zac demands. "Kind of unfair, brat."

Rolling my eyes, I mutter, "It's not because he had a thing for her. It's because I asked him and he blew it off like it was nothing. She was his fucking fiancée, Zac. And she lives on his property. While he's spouting off that I'm the only girl for him, he has one living on his property. I can be mad for a little while longer."

"Just not forever," Zac says, kissing my lips. "Promise me."

I huff. "Fine. Not forever, but for tonight, I am."

He winks at me. "It's good for him to have to suffer a bit. I think he's about to go crazy." His gaze drifts to the bar where Sebastian sits backward on the stool, watching our trio like a hawk.

Our eyes meet for a moment and his hard, blue-eyed glare flickers. I don't wait to see the remorse in them because I turn back to Zac. Zac's hands slide into my hair to tug down so I'm looking up at him. His lips crush mine in an all-consuming kiss. I moan into his mouth, loving the taste of liquor on his tongue.

"Fuck, sweetness," Leo growls behind me, pressing his erection against me. "You keep moaning like that and I'm going to flip your dress up right here. Is that what you want? To be fucked right here in front of everyone?"

Zac sucks on my tongue to keep me from replying. I rub my ass against Leo, desperate for what he's offering. I feel him fumbling at his buckle when I'm suddenly pulled from the yummy sandwich I was in.

Ford shakes his head. "Time to go, Lucky. Seb went to grab the Tahoe."

He doesn't allow me to argue. Simply tugs me through the small, local bar crowd and out the doors. I stumble along after him, buzzed from the tequila. The Tahoe pulls up and Ford drags me into the back with him. He tries to wrangle me into a seat belt, but I straddle his lap. I win our little war when my mouth meets his. On the other side, Zac hops up in front and Leo joins us on the bench seat. The Tahoe peels out and I fall against Ford. His hands grip my ass hard, pulling my cheeks apart.

"You going to let me in your ass one day?" Ford says in a husky voice.

"Mmm," I moan, rubbing against his hard-on through his jeans. "Is that what you want?"

"I think I can answer for everyone in this vehicle. We definitely want in there one day."

"One day," I mirror. "Why not tonight?"

He smiles against my lips. "You're not ready. But one day this perfect body will be nice and stretched."

Leo's palm slides up my thigh under my dress. "I bet you'd like to take two cocks at once."

I'm dizzy from the alcohol, but his words send a

shiver down my spine. "Two? Like one in my pussy and one in my ass?"

"Exactly," Leo says, his fingers grazing along the edge of my panties under my dress. "You think your body can handle two cocks? One for each hole?"

I nod because it sounds delicious.

"Or maybe," Ford growls. "Maybe you'd like two cocks in your tight little hole."

"In my pussy?" I gape in shock.

Ford bites my bottom lip and tugs before letting go. "We'd stretch you out and make you scream, Lucky."

"I want that," I purr.

"You're killing me up here," Zac grumbles from the front.

Ford laughs at him. "You're not dealing with the biggest tease on the planet grinding on your dick. Quit your bitching."

"Hey," I grumble. "I'm not a tease."

But, because he's being a dick, I tease him by dry fucking him all the way home. As soon as the Tahoe shuts off, the door gets flung open and I'm dragged into the arms of *him*.

Fucking Sebastian.

The heat drains away as cold fury ices my every nerve ending.

"We'll be inside in a minute," Seb growls. "I need to talk to Clo."

I'm irritated when all three leave me to this wolf.

Lying wolf.

Anger burns white hot inside of me. "Let me go."

Seb's grip tightens around my waist. The bastard has me crushed to his chest. "No."

The tequila turns me into a raging bitch. "Let me go or so help me I'll fire you, Seb. I'll fire you!"

The motherfucker laughs in my face. "Nice try, beautiful."

Why does he have to look so hot when he's being the world's biggest asshole?

"You're fired," I hiss. "We're done."

His features grow soft and he shakes his head. "While I love the fire in your eyes, I'm going to have to deny your request."

"You have to listen to me."

"I don't have to do shit except love you," he growls. "And that's exactly what I've been doing since you turned eighteen and I allowed myself the fantasy of having you. You're more than this obsession to me. You're everything."

I melt a little at his words. "You don't love me."

"Think what you want, Clo, but I know the truth. Rachel was a horrible, cheating girlfriend. She likes the idea of an us, but there is no us. But you and me..."

"And them," I say fiercely.

He nods at me. "Whatever makes you happy, makes me happy."

"I didn't like her hugging you," I grumble. "You're mine."

His features relax as he tentatively kisses my lips. "I'm sorry I hurt your feelings. I wasn't exactly sure how to tell you about her."

"I guess you'll have to make it up to me," I purr.

He grins wide and beautifully at me. "My pleasure."

I let out a scream when he ducks and tosses me over his shoulder. His hand pops my ass, making me squeal harder. I squirm in his arms as he carries me into his home. He doesn't stop on his trek until we're in the master bedroom, where I get tossed unceremoniously onto the bed.

"Hey," I grumble.

"Undress our girl," Seb barks out. "She wants us—all of us. At the same time. Anyone who's not okay with this, now's your chance to leave."

Leo yanks his shirt off and tosses it to the floor. His hard pecks flex, making his inked sparrows seem to come to life, and his abs ripple. "Not a fucking chance. I'm in. With Clove, I've always been all the way in."

I flash him a sweet smile, my eyes raking down his front as he sheds his clothes.

"Ford?" Seb asks. "What about you?"

Ford laughs. "Can't get rid of me that easily, buddy. Besides, Lucky would miss my handsome face if I left. Right, baby?"

I nod and smile at him. "Don't leave me."

"Never," Ford vows as he strips, revealing his tanned and toned muscles.

"You don't have to ask me, boss," Zac says to Sebastian as he starts shedding clothes. "Someone's gotta whip her bratty ass and keep her in line." He winks at me, sending tremors of lust ripping through me.

"I'm a bad girl. He's right," I agree, giggling.

Seb's eyes glint in a predatory way as he removes his clothes.

Four sharks swimming in the water around me. Each and every one of them looks as though he's ready for a bite. And, God, do I ever want to get eaten. Zac sits on the edge of the bed and pats the space next to him.

"Come closer, beautiful," he murmurs. "We all want to see your pretty tits. You have way too many fucking clothes on."

I edge closer to him on my knees. When I'm near him, his strong arm circles my waist and he hauls me against him. He bites at my breast through my dress. Seb steps over to us and savagely rips my dress away. The moment it's gone, Zac expertly undoes my bra. It, too, gets tossed away. Zac's hand slides between my thighs and he rubs at the wet spot that's now formed.

"Sometimes," Zac tells me with a wicked glint in his eyes. "Sometimes I steal your panties, wrap them around my dick, and come to thoughts of you riding my cock." He challenges me in his stare to balk at his words.

I meet his challenge head-on and shimmy out of my panties. With my eyes on his, I wrap them around his massive dick and stroke him. "Like this?"

He growls, yanking the panties away, and drags me into his lap. His palms find my breasts as he pulls my back to his chest. "Bad, bad girl, Clove."

His hands slip to under my thighs and he lifts me. I reach for his cock to guide it inside of me. He's huge and he's not gentle as he stretches me with his thickness. I let out a whimper when his hips thrust up, completely impaling me. Ford steps over to my left, a wicked smirk on his face. He tugs my knee over and then takes my hand. I grip his throbbing dick, my stare locked with his.

"Sweetness," Leo murmurs as he mimics Ford's actions. "You're so fucking hot, it's maddening. I wish you could see how pretty you look with your legs spread apart and your pussy stretched on Zac's cock."

His words send curls of pleasure swirling through

me. Zac thrusts up again, making me cry out. Leo helps me wrap my hand around his cock. I stroke both him and Ford at the same time.

"Now," Sebastian growls. "I'm going to apologize. With my tongue."

I lock eyes with him and stare at him in wonder when he drops to his knees in front of me. His mouth presses kisses from my bellybutton down toward my pussy. Zac grips my tits in an almost punishing way.

I'm completely at their mercy.

Seb's tongue lashes out at me like a whip. With perfect precision. He swipes his hot, firm tongue up my slit, seeking out my clit. A loud, embarrassing moan rumbles from me. His breath is hot on my sensitive flesh.

"Oh, Lucky," Ford chides. "You're going to have to learn to multitask." His grip on my wrist tightens and he wraps his hand around mine. With forceful jerks, he helps me stroke him. Leo's touch is gentler, but still urgent. I attempt to focus on them, but Zac keeps twisting my nipples and bucking up his hips. And Seb? He's trying to drive me to the brink of insanity with just his tongue.

It's too much.

It's all I ever wanted.

The urge to close my thighs around Seb's head is strong, but my guys are stronger. I'm kept spread open and at their mercy. Seb's tongue flattens against my pussy. Zac lets out a hiss when his cock inadvertently gets some attention from Seb's tongue.

"Can you taste me on him?" I whisper.

Zac growls behind me. "Dirty fucking girl. Look at you egging on shit you have no business egging on."

When I freeze, Zac laughs.

"I didn't say I didn't like it. You're our nasty girl. Your curiosity is hot as fuck," Zac says, pinching my nipples.

"Good, because I want you to lick us both, Seb. Make us come together over your tongue," I urge, making them all groan in union.

My words must give Seb the permission he's seeking because his tongue laves at my opening where Zac is thrusting in and out of me. I can't help but look down to watch him as he licks at my pussy. Every time his tongue swipes over Zac's dick, I clench in response. Seb must know how it turns me on, because he lifts his gaze to mine.

"Focus, Lucky," Ford growls, squeezing my wrist.

I shoot him a helpless look, but he's smiling at me. When my eyes drift to Leo, I cry out as Seb sucks on my clit.

"Oh God!"

He sucks on the nub so hard, my entire body shudders with need. It doesn't take long and I explode with an orgasm. Sebastian rises to his feet, his heavy cock bobbing out in front of him. Pre-cum leaks from his tip. I lick my lips, eager to have him in my mouth. He grabs a handful of my hair and roughly pulls me so his dick is within reach. Ford and Leo have both taken to using my hand with their own curled around each one to jerk them off. Zac grips my hips and pounds harder into me from beneath me.

"Open your mouth, Clo," Seb growls, his cock tapping at my lips.

I part my lips and he pushes inside. He's too big. Too thick. But I try for him. My mouth strains to accept him. I gag and slobber runs down my chin. Ford lets out a hiss before his cock throbs within my hand. Hot cum spurts out, hitting my side. Seb's grip on my hair tightens as he not so gently fucks my face. Tears stream down my cheeks as I try not to gag. I could tell him to stop and he would, but I don't want him to.

"I'll need some of this," Zac says, swiping his finger on my ribs. Then, his wet finger is at my asshole. "You talked a big game in the Tahoe. One day you'll let us fuck you here." His fingertip pushes past the tight ring. "One day. But tonight? Tonight, you're going to let me finger-fuck you here."

A squeal burns through my used throat that Seb continues to ravage as Zac firmly presses his middle finger into my ass. Ford's thumb gently caresses my hand that's still gripping his softening cock.

"Fuck," Zac hisses. "Fuck, you're too much, babe."

Seb's thrusting becomes crazed. I'm struggling to find air, but I want to taste him so badly. "Not"—thrust—"e-nough!"—thrust—"Never"—thrust—"enough!" He comes with a snarl. Thick, salty cum jets down my throat. I nearly choke on it, but he gives me a reprieve by pulling out and finishing on my face.

"Jesus," Leo rumbles. My hand that's wrapped around his dick aches. His cock seems to swell and then his heat is splattering me.

So much cum.

Another finger pushes inside my ass with the other one. My spine straightens as I cry out. Zac comes with a feral grunt, his heat rushing deep inside me. I think I might die from him filling me to the brim with both his cock and two fingers, but it's Ford who rescues me.

Gently, he pulls me off Zac's dick that still throbs with

his release. Cum runs down my inner thigh and the two invasive fingers pop out of my ass with a loud sound. Ford scoops me into his arms and then steals me away.

I'm so tired.

As my eyes flutter shut, I lean my cheek against his firm chest. "Where are we going?"

"I'm going to give you a bath."

"Just the two of us?"

"Believe me," he says with a chuckle, "I just saved your ass. Literally. As soon as Zac got hard again, he'd no doubt be trying to get in there. What I said tonight, I meant. You're not ready. Not tonight."

His words have relief flooding through me. I may want these guys with every fiber of my being, but I need a rest. I need practice. I need to be able to take more than two fingers without crying before I start begging for dicks in my every orifice.

"Thank you, Ford," I murmur, angling my head up to look at his handsome face.

"For what?" he asks with a smirk.

"For loving me."

His hazel eyes widen at my words, wiping the smirk off his face. He sets me on the counter in the guest bathroom. His thumb swipes away Seb's cum from my mouth and then his lips press sweetly to mine.

"It comes easily with you, Lucky. You're easy to love."

18

Ford Cross—Executive Weapons Specialist

Clunk.

I toss my tan Sig P320 on the table beside my H and K VP9 tactical. Both are still warm from this morning's target practice. Seb and Leo already left their weapons before heading to meet with a source a couple hours' drive from here that may have some information for us about the driver of the car that nearly hit our girl. It's warm in Seb's house and I yank off my hoodie before finding my range bag. Inside, among tools and extra ammo, I find my gun cleaning kit. I settle at the table and start taking apart my H and K. I unscrew the suppressor and sit it upright on the wooden surface. The smell of the oil when I pour some onto one of the cleaning cloths soothes me. I started cleaning guns for my old man when I was eight. Twenty-three years later and I still love this part almost as much as actually firing the weapons.

I'm long into my task of cleaning the firearms when someone clears their throat. I blink away my daze, locking my eyes on Clove. The mere sight of her in my T-shirt with her dark hair in disarray has my cock thickening in my cargo pants.

"Morning, Lucky," I greet, taking a moment to admire the hickeys on her neck. After her bath last night, I brought her back to the master bedroom where Seb had already taken up residence and was sleeping. We made out in the dark like two teenagers. Then, I sucked on her neck—marking her because why the hell not?—and fucked her sweet. She fell asleep locked in my arms with my dick nestled inside of her.

"Morning," she says, flashing me a warm smile before opening a cabinet and standing on her toes to reach for something.

I rake my eyes down her backside, loving the way her ass swells beneath the fabric of the T-shirt. Her legs are bare. Smooth. Tanned. And go on for miles. Even her feet are fucking adorable.

Clove is a walking, talking wet dream.

She sets a bowl on the counter and bites on her bottom lip. I arch a brow in question.

"You, uh…" she trails off and her cheeks turn bright pink. As though she's shy. I've been inside of her now and watched my best friends fuck her. What could she possibly be shy about now?

"Out with it, woman."

She lets out a nervous laugh. "You…you look super hot right now."

A chuckle rumbles through me. "Sorry to break your heart, beautiful, but my hands are all dirty. You're going to have to take care of yourself."

Her eyes widen in shock. "You're not going to fuck me?"

I pick up the suppressor and drop some oil onto it before cleaning it with a cloth. "Oh, I'm going to fuck you.

Every day if I can make that happen. But right now," I growl, lifting my eyes to meet hers. "Right now, Lucky, you're going to fuck yourself."

Pretty, plump pink lips part in response.

"Sit on the island and face me. I want to see what you get up to," I order, plunking the suppressor down on the wood table. "Come on. Show me what you've got."

She regards me with such an innocent look, but then it darkens as she finds her resolve. Her hips sway in a way that makes my dick respond with a jerk as she makes her way to the island. With her backside pressed to the edge, she grabs the counter and then hoists herself up.

Using my chamber brush that's in my hand, I wave it like a wand back and forth, indicating she needs to part her thighs. Her nostrils flare, but she obeys.

"My panties are still on," she says as though that will get her out of her task.

"Guess you'll have to get creative." I smirk at her. "Lose the shirt, though, Lucky."

She pulls off the material and tosses it to the floor. Her pale flesh is bruised on her hips and delicate neck. I may be responsible for the hickeys on her neck, but the ones on her hips are most definitely from Zac.

"What now?" she asks, dropping her gaze to the floor. Her dark hair falls in curtains around her face and over her full breasts that beg to be tasted.

"Forget I'm here. Do what feels good. Pretend you're alone."

Her brows furl together before she regards me with a troubled look. "I don't like being alone."

My heart squeezes in my chest. The urge to protect her, even from loneliness, is overwhelming.

"Remember not too long ago, before all this"—I wave my chamber brush in the air—"back to when I walked in on Seb in your room?"

Her nostrils flare. "We didn't do anything."

"But you wanted to," I challenge.

"I did," she breathes.

"So, go back to that day. Touch yourself like you wanted to."

Her small hand slides between her thighs and her middle finger rubs at her clit over her panties. I groan because she's so fucking hot. Spreading my legs apart, I lean back in my chair and stare at the delicious wet spot that now darkens her pink panties.

"Show me how wet you are," I growl, my eyes focused on her pussy.

She slips her hand into her panties and her knuckle pushes up the fabric as she seeks entrance into her pussy. A small gasp escapes her.

"One finger won't do, Lucky."

Her honey brown eyes dart to mine. "Two?"

"Three. Fuck all three until you're nice and juicy. Then show me."

She furrows her brows as she focuses on her task at hand. Literally. A whimper squeaks out of her. I sort of feel like a dick because I know she's sore. But if she's going to carry on a sexual relationship with four men all at once, then she's going to have to train her cunt to take four dicks like a champ.

My cock aches in my pants, eager to give her a little training right now. Instead, I go back to cleaning my guns, using my other senses to enjoy the way she touches herself. Her scent cuts through the oil smell and floods my senses, making my mouth water. Sweet moans resound from her as she slowly fucks herself with all three fingers. It's the sounds, though, that are maddening. The in and out of her fingers into her body make the wettest fucking sound on the planet and I'm so goddamn thirsty for it.

"Show me now," I demand, my eyes cutting back over to her.

Her eyes flutter back open and she pulls her hand from her pussy. She wiggles her fingers that glisten in the morning sun streaming in through the window behind me.

"Wet," I observe with a growl.

"So wet. All for you, Ford," she pants, licking her lips and gazing at me like I'm her everything.

"Clean your fingers off on your tits."

"Like this?" she purrs, swiping her slick fingers in circles around her nipple.

"Exactly. Do the other one now."

I'm about to instruct her to come let me have a taste when Zac rounds the corner into the kitchen behind her. His brown eyes gleam with wickedness as he prowls closer, dark hair dripping onto his bare chest from his recent shower. The fucker is hard as stone in his sweats. Images of him fucking her while I watch have my dick throbbing with need.

"My hands are all dirty," I tell him, wiggling my fingers on both hands. "And our lucky little clover is so desperate to get fucked."

Zac's nostrils flare and he licks his lips. "Looks like I showed up at the right time then."

She looks at him over her shoulder, baring her slender throat at me. The bruises there make me want to suck her harder the next time. Having them on her flesh all the time is an intoxicating thought.

"You came to rescue me?" she asks.

He shakes his head. "What I want to do to you is quite villainous."

"Your sweethearts left, Lucky," I tell her, dragging her attention back my way. "You're left with this dirty fucker"—I point to myself and then point to Zac—"and that kinky fucker."

Zac chuckles darkly. "He wants to watch me fuck you until you scream."

Despite his intimidating words, Clove is turned on. Her skin burns red and her lips part. Before she can utter a word, Zac has her yanked off the island and flipped back toward it. He bends her over, flattening her chest against the countertop. With rough movements, he yanks her panties down her thighs, ridding her of them. Her head turns so she can look at me. I have a nice side view of the deviant act. He pulls away to admire her ass, giving it a playful whap of his palm.

"Ow," she grumbles.

"If a slap to your pretty ass makes you say ow, then I can't even begin to imagine what you'll do when I put my big dick inside it," he growls, slapping her again, this time harder.

She whimpers. "You're going to hurt me?"

Zac's grin is wolfish. "You're going to like it."

"If it hurts too bad, you say my name," I tell her firmly, giving her an out if she needs it. "Zac's a freak, but he's not a monster."

She nods against the counter, wriggling her ass at him. "I know. Slap my ass again, Zac, and make me scream for you."

Well, fuck. She's proving she's more ready for us than we ever thought possible. Our bad girl likes it clean and dirty—soft and hard—rough and ready.

He pushes down his sweats until they're at his thighs. His heavy cock bobs out, bouncing up against her pussy. With a gentle but firm kick to her ankles, he forces her thighs to part farther. Rubbing his palm between her legs, feeling all that wet pussy just waiting to be punished, he rears back and gives her pussy a slap. Her body jolts and she cries out, but it's all from pleasure.

"Again," she pleads, needy as fuck.

I can't focus. It's mesmerizing to watch him with her, pulling out all the naughtiness hidden inside. Another slap makes her eyes almost roll into the back of her head.

"You think she's ready for me?" he teases, removing his hand and lining his cock up with her slit.

"She smells ready," I groan.

He slides between her pussy lips, gathering her juices, before pushing into her cunt. She slides her palms to the other side of the counter above her head and grabs on.

"I thought you were going to put it in my ass," she breathes.

"You'll just cry," he utters, his ass clenching as he thrusts into her.

She teases him back. "Happy tears."

"Shut up, brat," he groans.

She says no more as he fucks her into submission.

"She wants to cry," I tell him. "Give the girl what she wants, Zac."

His fiery gaze darts to mine before his attention is back on her. He pulls out, grabbing his dick in his hand. Then, he presses it higher. Her entire body tightens in preparation for him to breach her there.

"Relax," Zac and I both command at once.

Her body melts at our instruction. Dropping to his knees, he spreads her ass cheeks and swipes his tongue up her crease. She flinches and then cries out when he moves his mouth to the back of her thigh, sinking his teeth into her flesh—marking her. Swiping his fingers against her pussy, he gathers up her juices and uses them as lube to breach her puckered hole.

"Relax, Lucky," I demand, watching him fingerfuck her asshole, adding more digits and saliva from his mouth to get her all wet and ready for his cock. She's panting, her fingers clawing at the counter, her back heaving with her need for more. Rising to his feet, Zac gently pulls his fingers out of her ass and lines his cock up with her needy hole instead. With a hiss, he presses into her slowly, inching farther inside past the rings of muscle. A choked sound escapes her. Unlucky for little Clove, she had to offer her ass for the first time to the biggest dick in the bunch. Go big or go home, I guess.

A broken sob rattles from her.

"You know my name. Say it," I urge, giving her the out I promised.

Tears leak from her eyes and she shakes her head at me. Zac shoots me a feral look before grabbing her hip in a punishing way, inching the rest of his dick in.

"Fuck," he growls. "You're strangling my dick here, Clove."

His hips pull back and then he slams into her hard enough that she screams. Her knuckles turn white as she grips the counter, her entire body trembling.

"Say. My. Name," I snarl.

She's quiet as a fucking mouse.

So, Zac turns it up a notch. Fucks her ass hard and without apology. Her screams echo against the walls, sending fire through my veins.

"Fuck. Fuck. Fuck." Zac is a wild man as he pounds into her.

Another loud sob from Clove.

"Say it," I bellow. "Fucking say it, Clove."

She says nothing that will end the pain. She fucking likes it.

Zac reaches forward, gathering her dark locks in his fist, and yanks her up off the counter. He wraps his other arm around her stomach to hold her to him as he pistons his hips. She sobs, her feet locking around the backs of his thighs and her hands gripping the edge of the counter.

Tears stream down her face as he fucks her ass hard. He whispers many things into her ear, his grip on her hair tight. Eventually she seems to come undone, a heart-breaking sob rattling from her.

"Ford," she cries.

I slam my chamber brush down onto the table, ready to bark at Zac, but he's already releasing her and slipping out of her. Despite no longer being inside her, he comes against her back just above her ass.

"Such a good girl," he breathes into her hair. "Are you okay?"

She nods and turns in his arms to hug him. He squeezes her, kissing the top of her head.

"Do you hurt?" he asks.

Her shoulders shrug as though she's embarrassed to admit it.

"Go shower," I tell her softly.

Zac's fingers slide into her hair and he tilts her head back to look at her tearstained face. "Unless you're not done getting dirty."

He turns her head my way.

Fuck, she's so pretty. Especially a sobbing, just-fucked mess.

19

Clove Sterling—The Client

Fire burns through my ass and I can't stop trembling. It hurt. Sure, I talked a big game, but it fucking hurt. And yet…I didn't want him to stop. I'm depraved.

But these guys—no, these virile men—stare at me as though my depravity is something to be worshipped and adored. It has me tapping into my bravery. I'm not William's prissy girlfriend anymore. I'm not Dad's little media princess.

I am theirs.

Their woman. Their whore. Their dirty, dirty girl.

I don't know of any other women like me. A filthy slut who craves for four men to fuck her at every turn. In every hole. But here I am. Desperate for it. Trembling for it. Aching for it.

My ass hurts more than I can stand. I had to utter defeat. Zac whispered into my ear that he loved how beautiful and brave and strong I was, but he wanted me to throw in the towel. He promised, with time, that we'd work up to it and that eventually it wouldn't hurt. He begged me to say Ford's name and end it. For now. And then he whispered that he loved me.

Having that reassurance had me calling out the proclaimed safe word. And like it was silently agreed upon, he pulled out, finishing on my ass.

I failed them.

A few more seconds and he could have come inside me.

"Ford didn't get to come," I whisper, my eyes locked on Zac's.

His dark brow hikes up his forehead. "You've still got some game in you, brat?"

My lips tug into a smile. "Can't keep me down."

Zac winks at me, warming my insides. "Good girl." His gaze darkens. "Now crawl your way over to our friend Ford and show him what a good little cocksucker you are."

"Crawl?" I ask, my brows furrowing.

"Under the table." He nicks his head Ford's way. "Go on."

I stand on my toes and steal a kiss. For so many years, Zac was the one I was worried didn't like me. But his brown eyes shine with such heat and admiration it nearly blows me over.

And…he loves me.

"I love you too," I whisper against his mouth before breaking away.

My eyes lock on Ford's. His jaw clenches as he watches me intently. Slowly, I lower to my knees as Zac bends to pull up his sweats. I wince when a pain in my ass shoots through me. Then, I start crawling across the tile floor toward the table. I push past a chair and crawl until I'm between Ford's spread thighs. I rub my palms up his thick, muscular thighs and then set to unfastening his cargo pants. His dick is hard and springs free the moment I push his boxers down. He hisses when my hand wraps around his thickness. The tip glistens with his arousal. Leaning forward, I lick at his crown, loving the way he groans in response.

The chair behind me scrapes across the tile and Zac sits down. He stretches his bare foot forward between my thighs. I can't help but rock my hips, seeking the friction the top of his foot provides.

Zac carries on a conversation about guns. I pick up words like H and K and Glock and hollow point. Ford grunts, but his focus is mostly on me. It makes me want to steal all his attention. I slide my lips up and down along his shaft, trying not to gag each time his tip pokes the back of my throat. When Ford utters a "fuuuuck," I can't help but smile around his cock. My self-assuredness is cut short when Zac moves his foot beneath me, distracting me. Soon, I'm rubbing my pussy on his foot of all things, as an orgasm teases at me.

I attempt to slide Ford's thick cock down my throat, but the weird position under the table has me gagging hard. Hot tears leak from my lids, spilling down my cheeks, and slobber runs down my chin.

My guys make me messy.

I pull up and then try to take him again, choking. Zac's foot is being more aggressive and I shamelessly ride it, seeking the pleasure it offers. I'm just trying to take Ford down my throat again when my orgasm hits. A loud, guttural groan rumbles through me as I come. This must set Ford off, because his oiled fingers slide into my hair, gripping me hard. His hips thrust up, pushing his cock deep into my throat. The urge to gag is strong, but then he's coming. His heat surges into my throat and I do everything in my power not to throw up. I want to swallow him down and make this the best blow job he's ever had. Based on the sounds of pleasure emanating from him, I'd say I am successful.

At the last second, my throat constricts, forcing him out. Salty cum shoots across my tongue as he finishes. I swallow it down. Then, I kiss the tip of his dick.

He barks out a laugh. "Did you just kiss my cock?"

I crawl out from under the table and stand, frowning at him. "So? I wanted to kiss it."

His oily hands find my hips and he pulls me to him. I lean forward, drawn in by his hypnotic hazel eyes. He grips my throat, tugging me closer, and presses a sweet kiss to my mouth. "Lucky," he murmurs. "You can kiss my dick any time you want."

"For the record, you can kiss mine too, brat," Zac utters behind me.

Naked. Messy. And with cum all over me is how Seb and Leo find me when they walk in five minutes later. Never a dull moment around here.

20

Leo King—Open Source Intelligence Agent

Milo Grieves, a muscle for hire and getaway driver for low-key jobs. We now have a name and address for the driver of the car who tried to mow down Clove, but the fucker is in the dust.

A connection of mine in intelligence—an old military buddy who now works for the CIA—got access to the cameras from the scene. And by using a still image frame and face recognition tech, he got a match. But Milo has ghosted. Trying to find this motherfucker keeps leading us to dead ends.

"There's no way he's gone off the grid on a job that has only paid out a hundred and fifty K." Seb throws down the images and runs his hands through his hair. He's as frustrated and tired as the rest of us with this shit.

"Someone's tipped him off that we're looking for him. It's the only explanation that explains him going underground," Zac grunts, pacing the floor of Seb's office.

"Then we need to get the word out to him that we're offering money for information and that's it," Seb says, clicking on the video feed to his bedroom where our sweetness is sound asleep after being fucked *four* ways from Sunday. "What about everyone in Jack's campaign, Zac? Do they check out?"

Zac, who has finally stopped pacing the damn floor, comes to a halt by Seb. He's also watching the monitor as Clove shifts in her sleep making the duvet fall from her body, exposing her flesh to us. Fuck, no matter how many times we have her—taste her—it's never enough.

"Zac?" Seb barks, making me chuckle.

"Sorry. Shit, yeah. Marjorie is clean. She's dedicated to the Sterlings. The lower players do her bidding and all check out—college grads, wholesome families, dedicated."

"And Jack's new security team?" I fold my arms and rest my ass against the desk.

"They're more like hired dogs. Doing what they're told, don't ask questions type. Which makes me wonder if Jack is behind this, why not just have one of them try to run Clove down? Why outsource to someone outside of his circle and risk being discovered?"

"Maybe he didn't want to have someone that close and had them make Milo disappear instead? Because unless this fucker is hiding in a hole somewhere, it's looking more and more like a cleanup job," Seb voices what we're all thinking.

"So, what's next?" I ask the burning question.

"I say we bug the house and every car, and we keep our girl here with us until we have something solid to go on."

"Keeping her distracted with our cocks won't stop her from asking about Jack for much longer," Seb says, running his hands over his face.

A grunt sounds from Zac, and we follow his pointed finger to the screen. "Ford begs to differ."

A naked Ford comes into view as he ducks beneath the duvet between Clove's legs. Her back arches, making her tits bounce as he finds purchase with his mouth. Fuck, she's perfection.

"I can get on and off the property undetected. I'll plant the bugs." Zac nods and begins his pacing again.

"The house is swept once a month, always on the first of the month. That gives us twenty-eight days to gather as much evidence as we can to call out Jack before the bugs are found, and the jig is up," Seb tells us, scrubbing his palm over his face, stress evident on his tired features.

Zac stops moving, glancing between Seb and me, and then settles back on the screen.

"He could ask for her return at any time."

A rush of possession courses through my veins with his words, making every inch of me tense. My fists clench of their own accord. "He can fucking ask," I growl, "but he's got no hope in hell of that happening."

"Agreed," Seb adds in a fierce tone.

"I'll leave at first light," Zac confirms, pulling his shirt off over his head and waltzing from the room.

I turn all my attention on Seb. "When we get the evidence about Jack, this will kill Clove. One of us is going to have to break her heart," I remind him. "Bagsy, not it." I grin and slap a hand on his shoulder.

"Fucking bagsy? What are you, British? And nine?" he calls out to me as I head for the exit.

"Nine inches, motherfucker," I say in a fake British accent over my shoulder before heading out of the office just as Zac comes into view on Seb's monitor. I unbuckle my belt and shed my jeans to join Ford and Zac. For now, we can keep Clove in our bliss bubble for a little longer.

⟡

A week later…

A yawn echoes through Sebastian's office from my lips as I almost fall asleep watching the security monitors showing Clove, Ford, and Zac all cozy on the couch watching a movie, their limbs all entwined like vines. Seb's frowning at whatever the fuck he can hear through the headpiece he's wearing. We're going through the recordings from yesterday at the Sterling household. Zac managed to bug Jack's office while Jack was off doing more fucking interviews. Luckily, no alarm codes have been changed for the residence, so Zac was in and out without anyone knowing any better.

Throwing his headset off and onto his desk, Seb shudders and gets up to pace the floor.

"What's up?" I ask, trying not to smirk. I know exactly what's up because I had to go through Jack's office tape yesterday, and that fucker likes to keep his right hand active late at night.

"Marjorie. She's so desperate for Jack's cock it's disturbing." He shudders again.

Raising a brow, I wait for him to elaborate.

Placing his hands on his hips, he halts and furrows his eyebrows at me. "She's trying to entice him into her bed. It's like listening to someone's mom trying to get laid," he grumbles, throwing his ass back into the seat and picking up the headset.

"Is Jack going with it?" I ask, waggling my eyebrows and giving Seb a wink.

Shaking his head, he clicks on sound to come through the computer just as Jack begins explaining he's not ready to take that step.

"When I am, you know it will be with you. I need time." Jack's baritone voice filters into the room.

"Six years, Jack. She would want you to heal and love again," Marjorie tells him, and suddenly the air feels thick in the room. I squirm a little in my seat. It feels intrusive listening in on them for the first time since Zac placed the bugs.

"It's not just about me. I have Clove and the public to think about too, Marjorie. You know all this."

"We don't have to make it public right away, and Clove is an adult."

"Enough. We've already discussed this. Get me into the White House, and I'll make you First Lady. We're not there yet, and I'm the only one who's been doing what's needed to get us there."

My eyes cut to Sebastian, who glares right back at me.

"Good night, Marjorie."

"Night, Jack."

Sebastian slams his hand down on the desk, making the equipment rock. An alarm sounds suddenly on the security monitor of our property, drawing both our attention.

"Boundary breach," Sebastian snaps, bringing up the cameras for outside.

"Animal?" I query.

"Rachel," he growls, clicking to the cameras inside the house.

Zac is up at the front door, gun drawn with Clove standing behind Ford in the living room, all eyes on the front door. Marching out of the room, Sebastian is like a dragon about to breathe fire. It's past midnight and this bitch is proving she can't take a fucking hint. All week she's been making excuses to have Sebastian and Zac running around after her—a flat tire, a gas leak, anything she could think of to get them to her place.

Luckily, Ford and I kept our little sweetness preoccupied, so she hasn't noticed. She's going to fucking notice her at the front door at midnight, though.

Fuck.

21

Clove Sterling—The Client

Being wrapped up in the arms of Ford while Zac massaged my feet on the couch in a cuddle fest movie night was bliss until a weird beeping alarm sounded through the house, making both Ford and Zac almost catapult me from their hold to draw their weapons. Zac moved toward the front door while Ford ushered me behind him, backing me against a wall. And now we're all just standing rigid like a hellhound is about to burst through the front door.

Sebastian comes barreling down the hallway, his face a storm of anguish with Leo hot on his tail.

"It's Rachel. Relax," he grunts.

Ford snorts, clicking the safety on his gun, and tucks it in the back of his jeans—moving me to allow me to sidle up next to his side instead of his ass. His strong arm wraps around me, and we both train our gazes on Zac opening the door as Rachel pours inside on unsteady feet.

Throwing herself at him, her arms snake around his neck. *Viper.* Her face burrows into his chest like she has permission to be that intimate with him. My heart stampedes in my chest at their contact, ice water flushing through my veins reminding me that she knew my guys way before I did. I want to go over there, yank her off him, and toss her back out the door. I get a little satisfaction from the fact he doesn't reciprocate her affection. Instead, his eyes cut to mine across the room, a deep frown marring his forehead.

"What the hell are you doing here?" Sebastian demands, his tone cutthroat, making Rachel step away from Zac and drop her eyes to her feet.

"Someone followed me home. I got scared. I didn't know what to do," she says, sniffling.

"Where from?"

"The bar. It's the only night a week my mom gives me a break from—"

"Is Joey on the grounds?" Seb cuts her off, making her look up at him and nod.

"Motherfucker," Zac growls.

As if her words summoned this Joey person, another figure appears at the front door. Rachel rushes around Zac and pushes herself against Sebastian like she belongs there with him. I try to tell myself my jealousy is irrational, but it doesn't stop my fist tightening in Ford's shirt. His grip tightens around me, and he plants a kiss to the top of my head.

"Rach, are you in there?" the man shouts, tapping on the window of the front door before walking inside.

He slams straight into the brick wall of Zac, who grabs him by the lapels of his jacket and within seconds has him down on the ground, his arm twisted up his back as he presses his knee into his spine, restricting him from moving. "You picked the wrong house, motherfucker," Zac growls.

The guy looks drunk, his eyes heavy as he tries to survey the room from his position on the floor. "She left her purse," he slurs, trying to adjust his body by wriggling to no avail.

"Rick?" Rachel snaps, rubbing her hand down Seb's chest. "I thought it was Joey."

Pulling away from Ford, I march across the room, fire igniting my bones and aiding my confidence. Reaching them, I grab her hand from Seb's chest and walk her over to the dining room table before pulling out a chair. "Take a seat. I'll make you a coffee to help sober you up," I offer with a tight smile.

"I had no idea about this. I thought it was Joey, Seb, I swear." She yanks her arm from me and narrows her drunken gaze on me.

"I know her," Rick grunts from the floor and then groans when Zac increases the pressure on his back, moving his knee toward the guy's neck. "I've seen you on TV," he continues. He's looking at me, not Rachel.

"No, you haven't. Now shut the fuck up before I shut you up permanently," Zac growls.

My guys all communicate with their eyes, talking to each other without saying a word, and before *the not Joey* guy named Rick can say anything else, he's being hauled to his feet and ushered outside.

"Leo, stay with Clo," Seb orders. "Ford, take Rachel to her trailer while we drop this guy at the gate."

"Can Leo take me?" Rachel asks, making me squint my eyes at her and cross my arms under my chest.

"Why?" I snap, irritated that she showed up and has my guys cleaning up her mess. And now she wants to dictate who will be seeing her out?

"What's it to you?" she snipes.

My eyes cut to Leo, who looks like someone just castrated him.

"I'm not going anywhere," he assures me.

"Well, it looks like unfortunately, Rachel, you don't always get what you want," I say with a saccharine smile, cutting my eyes to Ford, who is grinning at me like a fool. "Get your shoes on, we're taking Rachel to her trailer."

22

Zac Stone—Electronic Security Agent

One week later...

They're buying favor. I shake my head as I look over the intel a contact was able to retrieve.

The money went to someone already in the White House. Jack is buying backers for his presidency campaign. In all the time I worked for the man, I would have never pegged him for being a corrupt motherfucker, but politics are toxic. I should have known better.

"So, we have enough to call him out on?" Ford fumes as he reads over my shoulder.

"We still need to link him to the driver, the money, something. Clo's going to need to see real evidence before we do anything."

"Why don't we just confront him while the bugs are in the house and hope he says something that will nail him? If she hears it from the horse's mouth..." he trails off.

Damn, that's not a bad idea.

"What if he doesn't say anything? Denies it all and demands we return his daughter?" Leo speaks our worst fear. There's no way we'd send her back to him while he's a suspect in all this, but we don't want this to turn into something else entirely.

"So, we do nothing like we've been doing this whole fucking time?" Ford scoffs.

Frustration chips away at us all one by one.

"I want Clo to be here because she chooses to be," I utter, frowning, "not because we're paid to watch her. We can tell her she's more than a client until we're blue in the face, but deep down, I can feel it in her words and her actions that it's in the back of her mind that we're still her security team. Paid by her father to keep her safe."

"She knows we're more than that. Our world starts and stops with that girl," Leo says, coming across the room to place a hand on my shoulder. "She knows we love her and this will all be over soon. We can start living our life how it should be."

"And how is that?" I ask, lifting a brow at him.

"Together for real. No temporary sleepovers, no fucking *Rachels* living at the end of the road. A place we all call home," Leo states, spilling his guts. "We're a five now."

"I want to skip to that part." Ford sighs. "I'm sick of worrying about what fucking Jack is up to."

Aren't we fucking all.

"Let's give it one more week," I tell them. "If we don't get something by then, we clear out the bugs, present the findings we have so far, and hope he gets talkative."

"We could make him talk." Ford grins evilly.

"That's a last resort," I tell him with a chuckle. "If you want to be sharing Leo's little fantasy with us, we should hold out on torturing our girl's father."

"Right," he agrees. "What about cameras?"

"What?"

"We bugged his office and cars, but what if we do cameras?" Ford suggests. "See what's going on, not just in his office, but the entire house. Marjorie's office, his campaign office, everywhere. Something's got to happen. Give us a clue where to go from here."

"It would take a lot of high tech equipment to plant cameras all over the place," I counter. "Small enough to not be detected."

"But it's not impossible. We have all the security codes to the house," Ford says, his features darkening. "His office and campaign office."

"We should run it by Seb first."

"Let's go do that."

⟡

The stress of the week is getting to me. I'm tired as hell and grumpy, too. So, when I hear giggling, it lights a match inside me. I should be working on acquiring the tech we need for our new plan, but after roaming the house and not finding Ford, I give up. If these dicks are going to ignore work for the day and play with our girl, then I'm going to play too. I prowl down the hallway on a hunt for Clove. She's in the master bedroom, curled up against Leo's side, looking up at him as though he hangs the fucking moon. Seb lies behind her, stroking her hair—his massive form dwarfing hers reminding me of a lion taking care of his mate. She's clothed, pity, and they're all being playful and affectionate.

It makes me want to storm in, strip her down, and turn her giggles into screams. My dick strains in my jeans, eager to do just that.

Neither guy makes any moves to rip off her silky nightgown, despite the way she rubs against Leo's hip, seeking out friction between her thighs. They're either tired this morning or they're deliberately holding out on her.

"Morning, Zac," she says in a husky voice. "Wanna cuddle?" The heat flaming in her eyes begs for more than cuddling.

Being the freak I am, I prowl into the room, a new agenda forming quickly in my mind. "I don't cuddle, brat," I lie. I'll do just about fucking anything with Clove. Even cuddle. She's soft and smells so damn good. Cuddling is definitely a must with her. "I do like getting my dick sucked, though."

She bites on her plump bottom lip. "I'll give you a cuddle suck."

Leo snorts. "A cuddle suck. What the hell is a cuddle suck?"

"I don't know," Seb growls, "but I fucking want one."

Emboldened by the sudden change in the atmosphere, she sits up and pulls off her silky gown, revealing her full tits to us. Her rosy nipples are peaked and hard as stones. I want to bite one until she screams and then give her relief as I seek out the other to punish.

"There will be no cuddle sucking this morning," I tell her, my voice firm and authoritative. "I want to watch you take two dicks at once."

Her eyes widen and her pretty lips part. "Like fuck and suck?"

Sebastian sits up, yanking off his shirt. "No, Clo," he says with a deviant smirk, his own dick tenting the covers. "He wants you to take both my and Leo's dicks at once." His hand slides between her thighs. "Here and here."

"W-What do you mean? L-Like both places at the same time?" Despite her nerves, her honey-brown eyes seem to liquefy with lust.

I walk over to the end table and pull out a bottle of lube. Wherever Ford went, I hope he picked up more at the store. We're going to need it.

Leo slides out of the bed and then sheds his clothes. His glimmering green eyes dart to mine as if to say, "Tell me where to go and I'm there."

I nod to the end of the bed. He sits on the edge before lying back. When he starts stroking his cock, he turns to look over at Clove. "Come have a seat, beautiful."

She sits up, shimmies out of her panties, and crawls down the bed. Seb and I both admire the nice round curve of her ass along the way. Before she gets to Leo, I motion for her to stop. Her eyes lift to mine, waiting for instruction like a good girl.

"I need to get you nice and ready," I tell her, my voice a low growl as I uncap the lube. I pour a healthy amount on my fingers before sliding between her thighs. My fingers easily slip between the lips of her pussy, teasing at her clit. "Now I'm going to finger you nice and good, brat. Make sure you're ready everywhere. But you have to stay still."

"Why?" she asks, her brows crashing together.

Seb chuckles darkly. "Because he said so."

"And if I don't?" she taunts back at me. "Are you going to spank me?"

I shake my head slowly. Before she can question me, Seb is on his knees and swats at her perfect ass. "No, he will."

She cries out in surprise. "Oh," she breathes, "I'll try to be good then."

Liar, liar.

Leo laughs as he lazily strokes his dick, watching the show. "And we all believe that, sweetheart," he teases.

While she's distracted by Leo, I slide two fingers inside her. Her moan spurs me on and I have the third one inside her the next breath. Slowly, I fuck her pussy with three fingers. When she whimpers, rocking against my hand to seek a faster pace, Seb doesn't disappoint. He slaps her ass with a punishing *crack*.

"Ah!" she cries out, her pussy clenching in response.

"Stay still for Zac," Seb reminds her, rubbing away the hurt on her ass cheek.

I fuck her with three fingers and then I add my pinky. Her tight hole protests against the strain of all four of my fingers to the knuckle. One day I think she could easily take two dicks in her tight little pussy. One day. But today she's going to take my four fingers, she's going to be still, and she's going to like it.

Her body quakes, earning her another spank to her ass. This time when she clenches, she whimpers.

"I feel so full and stretched," she moans. "It kind of hurts."

"It's going to hurt when you have two big dicks stretching out both holes," I remind her. "It's going to make you scream. And, Clove, it makes my dick so fucking hard when you scream."

She rocks against my hand, earning another strike from Seb. Without warning, I slide my fingers out of her pussy and push one into her ass. Her scream is of surprise. "Zac!"

I push another finger against her asshole, stretching her out here too. She's wiggling and groaning, all the while earning swat after swat from Seb. Leo has pulled his hand off his dick, no doubt turned on by the sight and seconds from coming. My own cock in my jeans leaks with pre-cum.

"Now you may go sit on Leo's dick," I say with a wicked grin as I pop my fingers out of her ass.

Seb spanks her once more. I slip out of the bedroom and into the bathroom to wash my hands. Quickly, I strip out of my own clothes and make it back to them. Clove has already straddled Leo and is fucking him slowly. Seb stands between Leo's parted thighs that hang off the bed, running his hand down Clove's spine in a reverent way. He releases her to pour lube all over his dick before rubbing it in. I climb onto the bed above Leo's head.

"You're going to scream, brat. So fucking loud. And I want to feel each one on my cock," I tell her sharply, earning her wild stare solely on me. "Are we clear?"

She nods, her tits bouncing as she greedily fucks Leo. He grips her tits and pinches her nipples. Sitting up on my knees, I take a fistful of her hair, guiding her to my big dick. Her tongue darts out when it's close, licking away my saltiness. I groan and grip her tighter, making her whine. She wraps her fat lips around my cock, desperately sucking at my thickness. My eyes meet Seb's over her prone body and he nods. He stops her rocking hips with a punishing hold on one side. The other hand grips his dick. When he barely presses into her, she moans around my cock, making it vibrate.

"It's going to feel good with both of them in there," I tell her. "And if it doesn't, you can bitch about it later."

Leo laughs from below me. "You're such an asshole."

I smirk at Seb. "Nah, Sebastian's the asshole. He's the one who's gonna make her cry."

As though to prove me right, Sebastian's brows furl as he presses into her. She screams around my cock. I hold her hair tighter, slightly thrusting into her hot mouth. Her teeth scrape along my shaft, making me hiss.

"Fuck, fuck, fuck," Seb growls. "This feels so fucking good. Clo, your body was made to take us."

As he drives into her, faster now, she slobbers all over my dick, forgetting her task with me. I like it, though. I like when she's distracted by the way they destroy her pussy and ass all at once. And when she's too distracted, I thrust hard down her throat, making her gag loudly. Fuck, she feels amazing.

Her ass must feel good, because Seb loses it all too soon. He lets out a snarl of pleasure before stilling. A string of curse words tumbles past his lips as he fills her ass with his cum. I almost come at the sight, but Ford walks into the room, distracting me.

"Jesus, assholes. I leave for thirty minutes and I miss out on this shit?"

Seb pulls out, his dick still dripping. "Tag, you're it."

I slowly fuck Clove's face as Ford strips out of his clothes in rapid speed.

"Want to see how pretty she is when she takes two dicks at once?" I ask him, pulling away from her sweet mouth and stroking her hair. "Flip her over."

Ford grips her hips, tugging her off Leo's dick, and then flips her around. "Looking so fucking hot, Lucky," he growls, his appreciative gaze roaming down her front. He grips her hips, sliding her back down on Leo's dick, this time slipping it into her ass that still drips with Seb's cum. Leo's palms grip her tits and he bites at her shoulder.

I stroke the hair out of her face and admire our girl. Her dark hair is in disarray. Honey eyes flare with wildness. Her pink lips are swollen and slobber runs down her chin from sucking my dick. What a beautiful fucking mess.

Ford wastes no time. He doesn't even mess with lube because her pussy still glistens with arousal and leftover lubricant. His eyes are on hers as he pushes the head of his dick past her slick pussy lips. All three of them groan at the intrusion. "Holy fuck," Ford hisses. "Leo, I like you, but right now, I fucking love you." He pushes her thighs apart wider so he can kiss her. "Lucky, you were made to take two dicks at once."

"So I've been told," she sasses, her words breathy.

They kiss for a moment and then he rises again so we can all admire our girl getting fucked by two men at once. I love the sounds coming from her body. The moans, the whines, the whimpers, the slurps coming from her lower half. Seb is hard again, watching the scene hungrily as he tugs at his dick. I yank at my own cock, desperate to mark her. When Ford pinches her clit in a punishing way that makes her scream and Leo groan at the way she must be squeezing him with her ass, it sets me off. I spill, hot and erratic, all over her tits. Leo wastes no time rubbing my cum in all over her perfect tits.

"Fuck," Ford hisses, thundering his hips hard. "Fuuuuuck."

He strums her clit like he's playing a goddamn guitar, setting her off like a nuclear bomb. She arches her back, screaming like a jet searing across the sky. Leo and Ford both make similar sounds of pleasure. Ford tenses and flexes as he comes. He's barely pulled out when Seb tugs him out of the way, resuming his position. Instead of sliding back into her used hole, Seb strokes himself to pleasure, splattering more cum all over her pussy. Using just his two knuckles, he rubs them on either side of her clit until she comes wildly again. Needing to see the damage myself, I slide off the bed and then tug on his bicep to move him out of the way. Gripping her hips, I push her up Leo's body, freeing his dick from her ass.

"Look at you, brat," I say, gripping her knees to spread her farther apart. "You're fucking gorgeous."

Ford and Seb both stand close to look at her used up body. Her pink pussy lips have turned red and raw, soaked with cum. With every ragged breath she takes, her asshole tightens, oozing little amounts of cum each time. I love the way her cunt is slightly parted between her lips, proving to us she just got fucked raw.

My dick is hard again as I imagine two cocks inside of her pussy rather than one. We'll need to practice like hell to get her ready for that. I hold my fist out in front of me, comparing it to her body. Imagining all the ways I could lube it up and make it fit. How I could prepare her to take two fat cocks at once.

"You're a motherfucking animal," Ford says, clasping my shoulder. "I'm going to take a shower, but whenever *that* happens"—he waves at my fist and then her used up pussy—"don't fucking start without me."

Clove's eyes are wide as she looks up at me, understanding my intent and motives without having to speak them.

"One day," I tell her with a wink. "Patience, brat."

She rolls her eyes, looking so goddamn adorable, but our sweet girl doesn't argue.

I may be dirty as fuck and kinky as hell.

But every last motherfucker in here, including this goddess of a woman, is right there with me.

Man, we make a great fucking team.

23

Clove Sterling—The Client

Two weeks later…

"Just like that, sweetness," Leo says from my peripheral.

I narrow my eyes and squeeze off a shot. The bang echoes loudly in the forest. Each guy has been teaching me how to shoot, but learning from Leo is my favorite.

He's a good teacher.

Plus, he's super affectionate and usually ends up praising me with kisses and hugs. The other guys, when we're shooting, just hand me new guns to try.

"Good girl," Leo says, taking my weapon from me and setting it on our card table we dragged out here. Then, he pulls me into his arms. "How are you doing?"

I look into his green eyes and frown. "I'm fine. Why?"

"You're just quiet the last couple of days," he says, worry etched on his handsome face.

Tearing my stare from his, I look past him into the thicket of woods. It'll be dark soon and the wind is picking up, warning of an impending storm. The weatherman predicted the rain would turn into sleet and potentially snow. I shiver against Leo's warm chest. His palms find my ass through my jeans and he squeezes.

"Clove."

I wince. "I just miss Dad."

He strokes his fingers through my ponytail. "I know you do."

"When can I talk to him? It's been weeks."

He stiffens. "You'll have to ask Seb."

Tilting my head back up to meet his stare, I search his expression for answers.

"Why? What's going on? What aren't you all telling me?" I demand, anger burning up inside me.

He lets out a heavy sigh. "We're just investigating some leads. And…" His features soften. "We don't think the car was supposed to actually hit you. Just appear to try."

"So, I'm not in danger? A stunt? Like you said before back at the cabin?" I shake my head, confused.

"Some shit points to your dad that we need to look further into."

Both my eyebrows shoot up. "You think my dad has something to do with this?"

"We don't know," he utters. "But telling him where you're at before we've had time to gather the intel we need, none of us is willing to risk it. You're safe with us."

"He's my father," I grit out. "Your theory is ludicrous."

"Look at the bigger picture, sweetness. He's so focused on his career and paying someone to attempt to run you over is good for his image—"

"Fuck you, Leo," I hiss back.

I push away from him and stalk away. He calls after

me, but I ignore him as I storm up to the house, leaving him to carry the guns and ammo back by himself.

How dare he? How dare them!

My father may be incredibly focused on his career, but he would never willingly pay someone to hurt me. He wouldn't even pay them to pretend. If this is my guys' intel, they've lost their touch, because it's inaccurate. Dad loves me.

I'm about to run up the steps to go into the house when a soccer ball rolls toward me from out of nowhere. I stop it with my boot and look around. A kid with shaggy, dark hair peers from behind the Tahoe, a curious look in his blue eyes.

"Hi," he says.

"Hey there," I say, then smile at him. "Where did you come from?" My eyes dart all around, looking for another car that could have brought this kid here. Nothing.

"Have you seen my mommy?" he asks, stepping out and moping.

I kick his ball back to him. "What does she look like?"

"Like an angel," he says with a grin. "Yellow hair and pretty smile."

Rachel? She has a kid…

"I'm sure she's around here somewhere. Want to come inside and get a snack while we wait for her?" I ask, swallowing the anxiety clawing at the back of my throat, and reach out my hand to him.

He walks over and slides his palm into mine. The kid can't be any more than six or seven. Why is he roaming about all alone? *He's not Sebastian's. He would have told me.* When we go inside, the guys are nowhere to be found. If I had to guess, they're all in Seb's office. They've converted it into a command center of sorts. It's where they discuss "my safety." All this time, I'd assumed it was from outside forces. But from what Leo says, they worry about my dad being responsible.

That idea sickens me.

I'm furious they'd even insinuate such a thing.

I'm fuming by the time we make it into the kitchen. I pick the boy up and set him on the island.

"I'm Clove. What's your name?"

"Seth." My heart almost falls from my mouth when he lingers on the Se…

"That's a nice name. What do you want to eat, Seth?"

He scrunches up his nose. "Do you have Oreos?"

These guys are health freaks. We definitely don't have Oreos.

"No, but I think there might be some strawberries left. You like strawberries?"

He nods and I set to pulling them out of the fridge. I cut them into halves and put them in a bowl for him. While he happily eats his strawberry pieces, I look at him. He's cute, which is no surprise if he's Rachel's son, but he doesn't look like her. His hair is darker and he just seems too sweet to be hers.

He's only half hers.

He's half someone else's. *Please don't be any of my guys.*

I shake away the thought that he might be Seb's. It wouldn't bother me if he was a father. What bothers me is we've been here for weeks and not one of these guys has mentioned Rachel has a son. It's like…they're hiding it from me.

Like they've been hiding the fact they're looking into my dad.

Sickness roils in my belly and I grab a package of crackers to munch on while I ponder my thoughts. I hear the front door close, causing my spine to stiffen. Poor Leo is about to get my wrath. Anger surges up inside of me as he rounds the corner.

But it's not him.

It's her.

Rachel.

"Mommy!" Seth cries out, waving to her.

All I can do is stare at her. With new eyes. She's not just the skanky ex. She's this adorable kid's mom. And this evening, she's not dressed like a hooker. She wears jeans tucking into her boots, a burgundy sweater, and a black puff jacket. Her blond hair has been pulled back in a ponytail. She walks over to Seth and kisses his forehead.

"There you are, baby," she coos. "I told you to play soccer out front. Why did you come inside?"

He points a red, strawberry stained finger at me. "Clove said I could. She got me strawberries." He holds up the empty bowl. "All gone now."

She pulls him off the counter and takes the bowl from him before ruffling his hair. "Why don't you go find Sebby and give him a hug bye. We're going to leave before the weather gets ugly."

"Sebby!" he cries out before running off.

Her mom smile melts away as she sets the bowl in the sink. She turns to glower at me. "You know," she says coolly. "We were supposed to be a family."

I freeze and gape at her. "He...Seth is..."

"What do you think?" She gives me a look that clearly means Sebastian is his father.

Recoiling from her words, I take a step back. My coat

is suddenly too hot. I feel like I'm suffocating. Not only does Rachel have a son that the guys failed to mention, but it's Seb's too. No wonder they didn't tell me. How could he be with my dad and me for six years while having a son back here being raised in a trailer at the bottom of his property line?

"If you hadn't shown up, Sebastian would have come to his senses. I'm not the woman he left all those years ago. I've grown up. I was ready to show him. Ready for us to be a family. But then you showed up," she hisses. "Fucking them all."

I wince at her words. "Stop, Rachel."

Her nostrils flare. "Stop? Why would I stop? You know, I was just like you once. I let them use me. Zac and Seb. Together. It's fun at first. Feels really good. But then, you soon realize you're nothing more than a fuck toy to them. A relationship with two men doesn't work."

She had issues with two.

I have four.

My expression must fuel her because she steps forward, concern flashing in her eyes.

"Oh, little girl," she coos. "You *have* been fucking all four of them. As hot as that is, I'm sure, where do you truly see that type of relationship going?"

Hot tears spring up in my eyes. My throat feels hoarse with emotion. "You don't know what you're talking about. I love them."

"Those boys are awfully generous with the L word. Seb loved me too. But then he left. I raised my son with the hope that one day he'd come back to me and we could finally be happy." She swipes away the tear racing down my cheek with her knuckle. "He came back. But he came back with you. Seb always did have a thing for a damsel in distress."

I step away from her, trying to hold in my emotions so I don't break down in front of her.

"I think you should leave."

"Oh, I'm leaving. Seb is moving Seth and me out. He has a new toy now, but the shine will wear off you as well, and then he'll put you out like trash too."

"I need to lie down. I have a headache." I swallow down the bile rising in my throat.

She smiles sweetly at me despite the waves of hostility rippling from her.

Suddenly, in a matter of twenty minutes, my happy world is shattered. Nothing feels sure anymore. And more than ever, I miss my dad.

I want to go home.

24

Sebastian Constantine—Chief Protection Specialist

"You got eyes on him?" I ask, dropping into my desk chair and swiveling around to where Zac sits on the sofa in my office.

Zac taps at his laptop screen. "He's at his office with Marjorie. They went in together."

Ford, from next to him on the sofa, leans over and peers at the screen. "Poor woman has it so bad for him."

I lift my brow. "Marjorie? No shit."

Both Zac and Ford nod.

"She clearly loves him," Zac says. "Now Jack? He tolerates her. Kisses her here and there, but he doesn't let her go much further."

Irritation bubbles up inside of me. He pays someone to run down his daughter for a publicity stunt and now leads on his PR manager. It's been embarrassing listening to her over these last couple of weeks. "Any leads on his next move? Is he done?"

"He's moved another large chunk of money to his offshore account, but I don't know what it's for. I'm assuming it's to buy more votes and favors, but if it's not…" Zac scowls. "Half a million."

"Half a million?" both Ford and I growl at once.

"The last stunt with Clove was a hundred and fifty grand. I can't even begin to imagine what kind of dramatics you can buy with half a million," Zac grumbles.

We're interrupted when the door creaks open. A dark-haired kid peeks his head inside.

"Seth?"

"Sebby," he squeals before running over to me. He throws his arms around me and I hug him back.

Guilt infects me. I haven't been by to see him since we came back. And the last time I saw him he was probably four when I'd come home for a rare vacation.

"How you been, kiddo? Staying out of trouble?"

"Yep," he chirps, pulling away from me. "I play soccer now."

"Soccer, huh?" I ask, darting my gaze over to Zac.

He wears the same uneasy expression I do. If Seth is here, then where is Rachel? I fucking hope Clove is still off shooting with Leo.

As Seth babbles about his soccer team, I shoot Zac a look that says, "Find Rachel."

He rises from the sofa just as Rachel steps into my office.

"There you are," she chirps to Seth. "I see you found Sebby."

He nods, grinning up at me. I can't help but ruffle his hair. He's a sweet kid.

"I think Leo should be back to clean guns any second," Ford says, rising. "Want to help me and Leo clean them?" He holds his hand out to Seth, who runs over to him without hesitation.

The moment Ford and Seth are gone, I stand and

storm over to the door to close it. Then, I turn my fury on Rachel.

"What did I tell you about just showing up at my house? You don't live here anymore, Rachel," I growl.

She winces at my words, clearly stung by them. Her eyes water with unshed tears and I immediately feel like a dick. "You told me to tell you if Joey comes back by and I saw his truck today. It was parked on the drive leading up to my trailer. We didn't wait around to see what he wanted or where he was at. Just jumped on the golf cart and came here. Jesus, Sebastian. I'm not some villain trying to cockblock you from your little princess."

Hastily, she swipes away her tears. Zac awkwardly pats her back. I walk over to her and regard her closely. Underneath the hardness and her pounds of makeup, she's tired and shaken.

"If he's harassing you, we should call the cops, Rach," I say softly.

She absently rubs at her neck. I know from her past that he used to choke her out when he was drunk as hell. More tears leak down her cheeks.

"I'm sorry," I mutter.

She throws her arms around my middle to hug me. Zac gives her shoulder a squeeze.

"We may not be together, but I still care about what happens to you and Seth," I admit. "I won't let Joey fuck with you two. Zac will go stay with you guys tonight and then in the morning we can go take a visit to the sheriff's office before you move on."

She lets out a sad laugh. "I've missed you guys. It's nice having people who care." Her body pulls away enough that she hugs Zac with her other arm.

We're just pulling away when someone gasps. Zac and I jerk our heads toward the sound. I can hear Ford, Leo, and Seth all laughing somewhere else in the house. But it's Clove who stands in the now open door, heartbreak written all over her pretty face.

Fuck.

It's not what she thinks.

She blinks away her tears and holds up her hand when I start for her. "No. I need some space."

"Clove," I call out.

But she's gone.

"Oh no," Rachel mutters. "Does she think?"

I scrub my palm down my face. "I'll talk to her. Zac, make sure Rach and Seth get home okay."

They both walk out of my office and I pace, wondering how I'll explain this to Clove. She probably thinks the worst. And that's my fault. If I had come out right after she learned who Rachel was to me, all this could have been avoided. But no. I had to try and preserve her feelings, banking on the fact Rachel would get a clue and leave me alone.

No such luck.

My phone rings, and I groan at being interrupted.

It's Jack.

"Hello?"

"Sebastian," Jack greets. "How are things?"

He calls every week, checking in, and each time it unnerves me. It makes me wonder if his security team is attempting to pinpoint our location. I try to keep our conversations short just in case.

"Things are well. President yet?"

He chuckles. "Don't I wish. Clove? Is she okay? She's

not mad at me, is she? I can't get her to respond to my texts."

Because we turned off her phone to keep her safe.

"Clove is fine. We take care of her," I assure him.

"Good," he breathes as though he's relieved. His sincerity is deceiving.

"Jack," a feminine voice calls out. "Your web interview is in ten minutes. We need to get you ready."

"Of course, Marjorie. Give me a minute," he says to her. Once she's gone, he lets out a sigh. "Women."

I grunt. "If that's all, I need to get off here and take care of something important." *Your daughter. I need to fuck an apology into her.*

"No, that's fine. Do your job. Her safety is my primary concern. Please have her call me, though. I miss her."

"I'll see what I can do," I grumble. "Goodbye, Jack."

We hang up and I stalk out of my office on a mission. I hear the shower going in the master and I wonder if I should just bombard her shower to calm her down. In the end, I decide not to. Instead, I walk into the dining room to find Ford cleaning the guns from Leo and Clove's shooting practice.

"Rach and Seth leave?" I ask, dropping down into the seat across from him.

"Yeah, Zac took them back just a minute ago." He frowns. "Clove knows. Leo went to talk to her."

I help him clean the guns and we fall into a broody silence for the next twenty minutes. There's no screaming or crying coming from the master, so Leo must be calming her down. It's better for Leo to talk to her until I can explain better. He always gets through to her in a way no one else can.

The front door opens and Zac walks inside, frowning. "Where'd Leo go? Was she that mad?"

"What?" I ask him in confusion.

Ford straightens. "Leo's showering with Clove."

Zac sprints off toward the back of the house. My hackles rise and my chair scrapes across the tiles as I go after him.

"What the hell?" I demand, trailing after him.

Zac storms into the bedroom. Leo sits on the bed with a towel wrapped around his waist and his phone pressed to his ear. Zac rushes into the bathroom and then roars with fury just as Ford flies into the room.

"Tahoe's gone," Ford barks out. "Where's Lucky?"

Leo hangs up on his call and stands up. "She was in your office with you," he snaps. "Rach said you two were talking."

"For five minutes," I hiss. "Where the fuck did she go?"

Zac exits the bathroom and his jaw clenches. "She left. She took the Tahoe and fucking left."

Ford jerks open the end table and then kicks it shut. "Her purse is gone. Fuck. Seb, she left!"

"Call Rach," I order, "we need her car."

Zac is already pulling up his phone app. "Tracker shows she's twenty-five miles from here. Goddammit. She's hauling ass too. The weather is turning shitty. I was just out there."

Panic makes my heart stutter. This is all my fucking fault.

"Stay here," I bark at Zac. "Find out what you can. Ford and I will follow her. Have Rach have her car ready. Rach's dumbass ex is hanging around, so make sure you have eyes on her just in case. We'll find Clove."

"What do I do?" Leo demands.

"Put some fucking clothes on and try to get Clove on the phone."

Ford and I dart out of the room, yanking our coats off the rack along the way. We rush outside into the blistery cold. Pellets of ice sting my face. Rach's pussy-ass little Chevy Malibu will be a bitch to drive if the weather gets worse. Thank fuck the Tahoe is outfitted with good tires and four-wheel drive.

We waste a precious ten minutes running up the drive to Rach's trailer. Luckily, she's waiting with the keys in hand.

"Be careful," she calls out after me. "*Please* be careful."

"I will," I grumble as I yank the car door open. "Zac and Leo are nearby if Joey shows up."

I squeeze into her tiny ass car and turn over the engine. Seconds later, we're cruising down the drive and then onto the main road. Ford now has the tracker app open on his phone. He points me east. We drive down the dark highway as the sleet turns into snow. The Malibu slides a bit on corners, but I'm able to keep it on the road. For nearly thirty minutes we drive until we pull into a motel.

"Bingo," Ford mutters, pointing at the Tahoe.

I whip into the spot next to it. We both jump out. The vehicle is empty and the keys are sitting on the seat.

What the fuck?

"I'll find out which room she checked into," Ford barks out before stalking into the office.

I pace around the Tahoe, making sure I didn't miss anything. My phone rings and I answer on the second ring, putting it on speaker.

"Talk to me," I growl.

"She called her dad," Zac hisses. "Not from her phone but from a pay phone at a hotel."

"She's not here," Ford bellows, storming over to me. "The clerk said she took an Uber from here."

"An Uber?" I demand. "To where?"

"Obviously back home," Zac says coolly.

"You know how expensive it would be to have an Uber drive her hours back home?" I snarl. The icy wind whips around me and snow flutters against my face.

"Real fucking expensive," Ford utters as he opens the Tahoe driver's side door and peeks inside. "But she's Clove fucking Sterling. She's loaded."

"We need to get her," I bite out. "Now."

"Go after her, man," Zac orders to me.

"The Tahoe needs gas, but then I can come get you guys," Ford tells Zac. "We won't be far behind Seb."

"We're already on our way," Zac informs me. "Rachel's new guy Rick showed up and we borrowed his car."

Borrowed. I bet her new dickhead boy toy loved Zac and Leo stealing his car. They'll get over it, though. Our primary focus is on getting Clove back.

"Seb," Zac barks out just as I slip back inside the Malibu. "We're going to get our girl back."

We fucking better.

25

Clove Sterling—The Client

When the Uber rolls to a stop in front of the iron gates leading up to my house, the warm, familiar feeling I was hoping to wash over me in welcome is absent. My thoughts remain lost to my four guys. They'll be going out of their minds with me just up and leaving. In the heat of the moment, I was angry—too hurt by Rachel's implications. And then to find them embraced in such an intimate way? I let my rage guide me and now I'm here. I don't know if it was the right thing to do. If my guys had allowed me my cell phone, they could have called me, and I could have explained that I needed some time to let all the new information sink in. To allow my insecurities time to adjust to my new life. To accept that maybe I'm not special to them…that I'll also have to learn to share them.

No.

I couldn't ever do that.

It may make me a hypocrite, but it was just never an option. I can't share them. It would be too painful. They're mine…or at least I thought they were.

I need to talk to my dad. To clear up any suspicions the guys have toward him.

"Identification?" some broad guard I don't recognize barks to the driver.

Opening the car door, I step out and approach him. "I'm Miss Sterling, your boss's daughter. I live here. Please open the gate."

The man's brows tug down, making a scar slashed through his right eyebrow tug up the eyelid, making him appear menacing. "Miss Sterling, we weren't told to expect you."

"Doesn't change the fact I'm standing here. So, again, please open the gate and inform my father that I'm home," I say testily. The long day has exhausted me, physically and emotionally, and I want to curl up and cry.

"Right away, ma'am." He nods and goes to the little visitor box to press the button that opens the gate. "I can take you up," he informs me, handing the Uber driver a bunch of bills and jerking his head to dismiss him.

Gesturing with his hand to a golf cart, he eyes me expectantly. I shake my head to decline. "I'll walk. I could use the air."

The truth is, I need the short time to hash over what it is I'm going to say to my father. Up until now, all I could think about was Rachel's words rattling around my brain, making a hole open up in my chest. Her seemingly insignificant rant had more impact than I would've liked, making me feel foolish.

I regret offering to walk almost straight away. It's too cold. I pull my coat tighter around me to try and bring heat to my skin as the house comes into view. I'm nervous when I shouldn't be. This is the house I was raised within. It's always been my haven, yet it feels oddly unfamiliar now.

My feet protest the walk up the winding driveway, blisters rise on the soles of my feet, and I sigh when I reach the steps leading to the house. Marjorie comes rushing out to greet me. She hurries toward me, throwing her arms around me, catching me off guard and forcing me backward on my feet. She's never this affectionate. Perhaps she missed me?

"Clove, honey, whatever are you doing here?" she coos into my ear before pulling back and looking behind me. "Are you alone?"

"Yes, I needed to come home," I say with a sigh, walking around her and up the steps to go inside. The door clicks closed behind us, and I push my shoes off before dropping my purse and coat on the rack.

"Is Dad home? I left him a message, but I was at a pay phone and he may not have listened to my voice mail." My ears perk, listening for any noise, but only silence greets me.

"No, I'm afraid he's not and won't be returning until later." Marjorie offers me a pat on the back like I'm an abandoned child.

"I'm going to go to my room to rest for a while," I tell her, feeling her eyes on me with a million questions I know she's dying to ask me. Marjorie hates surprises and not being in the know. She is meticulous with our lives and anal when it comes to constructing our family image to the public, so she will be on damage control to pay the Uber driver off to keep his silence about his passenger for the night, and to make sure no paparazzi caught me on my travels home looking like a train wreck.

Pushing into my bedroom, the scents of my old life burst over me, reminding me of how much change has happened in such a small amount of time. Brushing my fingers over the dresser, I note a little film of dust lacquered upon it. They must have told the cleaner to stop coming in here. I am forgotten, out of sight out of mind. I hate my thoughts. They're weak and pitiful, but I feel like I was cast away and life went on for my father. All the panic and worry for the threat on my life one minute and then as soon as I was out of the way, he went back to a politician, a product of what the people want. A man without worry. The man who is on his way to the White House.

Where was the father hidden between the layers of this man who once was the sunrise and sunset for his little girl? Leo's words echo inside me. *"He might be involved, sweetness."*

I shake them away, stuffing them so deep down that they don't exist to me anymore. They can't be the truth. I refuse to believe them even if my guys have proof. It would take my father pulling out a gun and shooting me point blank before I could ever think my soul could be so cursed that even my father could take it from me.

Sitting on the bed that doesn't feel as soft or welcoming as Sebastian's, my foot taps mindlessly on the wood floor. Will I get past this deception of Seb having a child with another woman? Do I have a right to be this mad with him? With them? They all knew and let her have this pocket of information to take out and drop on me at her choosing. I wasn't prepared. I was naïve and she could see it written all over me, exploiting it. The anger bubbles inside my chest once more. Tears of sorrow and fury wage war inside me. I hate that she has a part of him and can offer him a normal life without this chaos and media storm waiting to swarm. I resent her and hate myself for it. A tap on the door draws my attention and Marjorie opens it, stepping inside without prompting.

"I made you a cup of chamomile tea," she says with a smile, placing a china cup on my bedside table. "We gave the staff a long vacation just to keep an eye on who is coming and going on the property with threat levels being high." She lingers, folding her arms over her small chest. The cardigan she wears is an awful toffee color and makes her skin look washed out. She could be pretty if she tried, but she ties her long hair into a low bun and opts for oversized glasses rather than contacts and minimal makeup as to not draw attention to herself. I know she's in love with my father. I can recognize it now—the looks, the longing, the need. I feel bad for her in that respect, because my father will never have time to love anyone else. And when he is ready to remarry, he'll look for an accessory, a woman who will look good to the public. Maybe a charity background or a wealthy, wholesome family. Marjorie has no family. We're her family. My father's career is her entire life's work. Her blood, sweat, and dreams are all wrapped up in another's success or failure.

I pick up the cup and sip, trying not to wince when the bitter twang of an added lemon hits my tongue and explodes over my taste buds. "It's perfect, thank you," I lie, offering her a tight smile.

"So, what brings you home with no forewarning? Your father said you would be away at least another month."

"Things change. I don't believe I'm in any danger. There's no motivation for someone to want to hurt me. I'm no threat to anyone." I shake my head and laugh, but it's awkward and makes me squirm a little when her face remains stoic.

"Someone tried to run you down," she reminds me. "I would hardly say you're not in danger. Something like that can have so many ramifications. The psychological effects can be life-altering."

Quirking a brow at her, I snort and place my cup back on the dresser. "I'm fine, Marjorie, just fed up with living like a hidden princess. I want this over with. I refuse to live my life in such a way. My father is going to be heading for the White House, and surely I can't be hidden away forever."

My head swims a little and my heart begins to slow inside my chest. Smacking my lips together, I sink my teeth into my bottom lip and feel nothing. It's numb. What the hell?

"You look tired. I'm going to run you a nice bath. Drink your tea," Marjorie insists before going into my bathroom. I turn to the cup and reach out, but my limbs are awkward and long, heavy, uncooperative. The china cup topples from my unsteady grasp and crashes to the floor, shattering like my sanity over my wood panels. Fog clouds my mind, soaking me in its damp mist. What's happening to me?

"You know," Marjorie's voice sounds distorted. I can make out the sound of running water and her shadowy figure standing in the doorway to the bathroom. "Jack was born to become president. With a little push in votes, he could have it all. This," she says, gesturing with her arms at me. "You coming home alone like this was fate. I planned on asking Jack to bring you home. I was going to show him the distasteful images I had my guy taking of you."

"What?" I slur, attempting to stand, but my legs become Jell-O. I fall back to my ass on the bed.

"You think I would allow those men to take you off without me keeping tabs on you?" She lets out a mocking laugh. "You're a product, Clove. Your very being can make or break your father. A scandal right now when he's this close would destroy him. *Us*. I know you're fucking those men like a disgusting whore who gets passed around like a bottle of cheap whiskey. Everyone gets a swig and buzz. They devalued and disgraced you. Is it them who had you running back here? Were they done playing pass the parcel?"

"Stop," I snap, my thoughts swimming in mud. Her words are making sickness crawl up my throat and invisible dirt stick to my skin, covering me in shame.

Who is this woman replacing the Marjorie I've known nearly my entire life?

Walking over to me, her face comes so close to mine I can smell the cigarettes on her breath. I didn't know she smoked. Her lip curls as she studies me, her face saying all the things her words never have. I'm a problem. An insignificant bug that's flown into her home that she needs to get rid of. Humming begins pounding in my skull.

"What did you do to me?" I weep, trying to clasp onto her but grasping air.

"I added something to your tea to help you relax in the bathtub, and you've been struggling to cope after the near miss. And then, of course just breaking up with your future husband William. Everything combined just took its toll on you. The many nights I found you crying in your bedroom. My heart breaks for how lost you were, and I couldn't do anything to help you. You were just so broken."

My stomach twists at her words.

"Marjorie," I breathe.

"You were so depressed and we should have seen this coming. I mean, you were never the same after your mother's sad end. This was inevitable."

"Don't speak of my mother," I heave out, losing my breath.

"Your mother was a sacrifice to a greater cause. With her tragic death, sympathy poured in, launching your father's political career. Of course the idea of getting her out of the way was so I could take her place. I didn't think it would take this long. Once you're gone, though, he'll find comfort in my arms and together we will start anew."

"No." I try again to stand but fall to the floor. Tiny pinpricks cut into my knees as I land on the broken china. The bedroom door opens and heavy footsteps pound over the wood flooring, coming to rest at where I'm struggling to right myself. Strong hands reach under my armpits and tug me up, before I'm thrown back onto the bed like I'm weightless.

The air whooshes from my lungs as my limbs flail around me, completely detached from my will. My motor skills are shot, and my body feels weighted with lead.

"Strip her and move her to the tub," I hear Marjorie instruct. The man from the front gate comes into my misty vision, his lips in a thin line as his hands mistreat me.

"Stop it," I bark, but it's weak, the volume not computing from my brain to lips.

"Don't rip them, idiot. It needs to appear as she undressed herself," Marjorie snaps. Cold air creeps over my exposed flesh as he removes my clothing. Tears build in my eyes and fall to my cheeks as humiliation stains my soul.

"Shame we couldn't take another route with this."

The guy sneers, lifting me up to tug my shirt from beneath me. Attempting to fight him, I thrash my body and end up kicking out and gaining purchase. He howls out and growls, "Bitch." His backhand whips out and collides with my cheek, rattling my teeth and making fire explode over my face.

"Don't mark her, you imbecile. Get her into the bathtub if you think you can handle a drugged little girl on your own," she mocks cruelly.

Thick fingers grab at my flesh, digging in and ripping me from the bed. I'm scooped up into an unwelcomed hold, a hard chest I don't find comfort in, the touch of a man I don't know breathing over my naked skin. This is all wrong. Emotions clog my throat as he marches me through my own bedroom. Attempting to struggle is futile. His grip is painful, and whatever was in that tea has left me weak. Cool water consumes my body with a splash, cocooning me in its watery depths as he drops me like a stone in the ocean. Gasping for air as my head surfaces, the man's face sneers above me. His square chin juts out, and slimy eyes creep over my body. Roughly, he pushes down on my shoulders. Maddening panic races through my muggy mind, causing me to call out in incoherent screams, which allows water to infiltrate my mouth.

He's going to kill me. Drown me and make it look like I did this. My guys will blame themselves. They will think I did this because of the truths I learned from Rachel. They will never know how much I love them. How none of that stuff matters when you're faced with your own mortality.

I was so stupid.

I had everything and instead of reaching out and

grabbing hold, I let pride break me. I let outside interference sway me. Allowed Rachel to infiltrate our happy bubble and burst what we built.

I'm so sorry, Seb. And Ford and Leo and Zac. My heart aches.

"Such a shame you took too many pills and fell asleep in the bath. Suicide is an epidemic lately." Marjorie's voice penetrates through my drowning ears as I fight to surface.

I can't go out like this. My guys need to know.

My hands ball into fists, the nails piercing the skin as I fight for my life, willing my heavy limbs to work, to move, to save me. The blood seeps from my skin. *Try and convince people this was suicide, bitch,* my mind screams.

I try with every cell in my overwhelmed fatigued body to fight to live, but the strength and water overpower me. I sink deeper, beneath the heavy weight of the drugs and the water. The arms submerge me harder, forcing me to stay under, keeping me there until I'm choking, weakening, losing. The cold liquid chases down my throat, stealing my life from me.

Darkness consumes me.

My life had finally just begun. They made me theirs, and I ran.

Now I'm dying…

I'm dying…

I'm dying…

I'm dy—

26

Sebastian—Chief Protection Specialist

There's no one at the gate when I arrive, which makes my muscles ripple over the bones beneath them. Even if Jack isn't at the property, there's always a guard at the gate. I jump from the vehicle and check inside the small security booth, hitting the button for the entrance to open. Climbing back inside the shitty Malibu that almost choked out halfway here, my fingers drum rapidly on the steering wheel, willing the gate to move fucking faster. I check my rearview mirror, but the guys haven't caught up yet. Hopefully they'll get here soon.

I've never felt anxiety like what she's put me through in the past several hours. When Zac said she called her father, my heart almost exploded in my chest. I knew I loved her, but I don't think I truly grasped just how damn much until the prospect of not having her became a real possibility. She witnessed something innocent with Rachel and us, but who fucking knows what shit Rachel has been whispering to her, making it out to be more than what it was.

This is all so new to Clo, and the circumstances so abnormal. I clearly haven't shown her just how damn much she means to me. How fucking deeply rooted she is inside me. She is in the very essence of who I am. I can't bear to think of a life where she's not at the center of it. I need to tell her and prove to her that it's only her for us. Make her understand that no one else compares or matters. Let her know that Rachel is as insignificant as a mouse finding its way inside your house.

Finally, the gate clanks open and I hit the accelerator, punching forward the small tin can, pushing its limits. Screeching to a stop in front of the house, I jump out and race up the steps. I wiggle the handle to no avail. It's locked. No surprise there. I didn't think to bring keys with me in my mad rush out of there.

Banging my fist against the wooden panel gets me nowhere. Is no one here? I take off around the house and try each door and window, coming up empty. Garage. It has a code lock on the outside. My heart thunders in my chest as I approach the panel and input my old code. When the red light beeps to green, I sag in relief.

It's eerily quiet when I make it into the main house. No staff litters the halls. My shoes creak over the polished floors, causing an echo. The tiny hairs rise on the back of my neck when I hear a faint sound coming from upstairs. Jack wouldn't hurt Clo. I believe that deep down. Not with his own hands anyway. She's going to be in her room sulking, and I'll scold her for leaving and being reckless and then she will cry and shout at me. I'll fuck all the hate out of her until she's brimming with only love. We will all laugh about it on the way back to my house and decide she's never allowed to take off again. She has to stay, not because she's our job, but because she's ours period. Taking the steps two at a time, I follow the hum of voices to Clo's bedroom. The door gives way under my hand. A cold dread saturates my body before I'm even inside.

Fury unfurls in my chest as I enter. An overbearing ache pulses in my gut as I see straight to her bathroom through the open doorway. There's some big fucker leaning over the bathtub and Marjorie looking down to whom he has submerged. A roar, wild and unrestrained, tears from my lungs as I take off toward him, colliding with his middle and taking him off his feet. We crash through the glass wall of the shower, shattering the glass and hitting the cold tiles. Marjorie's shouts echo around me, but all I see is him and the red mist clouding my mind. The guy hits his head with a thud and becomes limp beneath the weight of my body. Rushing to stand, ignoring the pain of glass shredding my flesh, I stumble to the bathtub.

No. No. Fucking no.

Water splashes everywhere as I step inside and pull my girl up from beneath the water. Her lips are turning blue, and she's as white as a sheet.

No, no, no, no.

"Baby! Baby, it's okay, I'm here," I weep, pushing the dark strands of her hair from her cheeks and dragging her limp frame from the bathtub. Her naked body sags in my hold and fear like nothing I've ever experienced roots itself inside me like a plague, consuming me.

Focus, Seb.

CPR.

She needs CPR.

I won't let her die on my watch.

Before I can act, hot, white pain tears through my

back, making me almost drop Clo and collapse from the agony of it. Marjorie screeches as she attempts to pry the shard of shower glass from my flesh so she can stab me with it again. Placing Clo onto the floor, I swing my elbow around, finding purchase with Marjorie's stomach, robbing her of breath. She staggers backward, giving me time to advance on her.

"You fucking cunt," I roar. "It was you this whole time."

I should have known. I should have connected this big fucking dot.

She snarls at me. "She's a whore! She will tarnish all the hard work we've put into getting to the White House!" Her eyes are narrowing on me into evil slits.

How could I not see the dormant beast lying in wait within her?

"You hired that motherfucker to run her down?"

"Milo wasn't hired to kill her," she sneers. "Just to appear as a threat. It would have been enough too, but the little whore had to go opening her legs for you perverts. After everything I've done to get us here, she won't ruin this. I won't allow it."

"You're fucking crazy," I bark. "You really think you'd get away with this?"

A weird cackle rips from her lips. "Milo is at the bottom of the ocean, and once you bleed out, you'll join him." She attempts to swing out at me like a rabid cat.

I rear my fist back and smash it into the side of her head, knocking her clean out, her small frame collapsing with a soft thud.

Too much time wasted on fucking crazy.

I drop to the floor beside my girl and tilt her head

back, pinching her nose. I breathe into her lungs and then begin compressions.

One…two…three…blow…

One…two…three…blow…

"Please, baby," I beg. "Please, baby…don't leave me. You can't leave me."

27

Ford Cross—Executive Weapons Specialist

Driving up toward the house, we see the garage door open and head straight for it. The energy thrumming in the air shrouds around me like a storm cloud waiting to erupt. Every muscle in my body aches from being rigid since learning our girl took off on us. There's this pit in my gut like a black hole swallowing all the happiness from these past weeks into its cavernous pit.

We all exit at the same time, me from the Tahoe and Leo and Zac from the Mustang they borrowed from Rick. They're both armed already, and I fling open the backseat of the car to grab my own weapons. Once we're ready, in less than thirty seconds later, we take off in a jog into the garage and through to the house.

"She'll be fine," Zac barks for the thousandth time since he came back to get us, reading our minds because he feels it too. A shift in the air, the dread weighing us all down. We shouldn't have let our guards down. We let her slip through our fingers. If anything happens to her, I'll never forgive us. "She'll be fine," he says again. But there's a tone to his voice I've not witnessed before. Fear.

"Hello?" Leo calls out when silence greets us inside. "Hello?" he tries again as we each take a room, searching them.

"Up here," a desperate call penetrates the air from upstairs. Sebastian.

I'm closest and first up the steps. A drumming pounds in my ears as I race to Clove's bedroom. The world spins when I go inside to see her limp body soaking wet on the bathroom floor.

Blue.

So fucking blue.

What the actual fuck!

Sebastian leans over her, his huge palms pumping at her chest.

No, no, this isn't happening. This isn't real. She's not dead. This isn't real.

I'm barged out of the way as Zac and Leo race past me and take over for Sebastian. Tears drip from his eyes as he watches them frantically work on her.

One…two…three…breathe…

One…two…three…breathe…

"Ford, in the garage there's a medical cabinet with a defibrillator. Go now," Zac orders, jerking me from my state of shock. His voice is more desperate than I've ever heard him.

My feet stumble and my heart leaks its essence into my chest cavity when I witness no life coming back into the woman we love. Lead fills my bones, making them heavy and off-kilter.

"Now," he barks, jolting me into action.

I rush through the house to the garage, locating the huge white cabinet standing from floor to ceiling. Inside is everything you may need in case of emergency. I grab the defib and take off faster than I've ever moved in my life back to the bedroom. They've moved her now to the bedroom floor. Leo snatches the box from my grip and begins placing the two pads onto Lucky's chest. My eyes trace over every inch of her, sending up a silent prayer to a god I'm not even sure I believe in.

She's so pale. Her lips are darkening to an awful shade of blue. Crescent blood moons mark the skin on her palms, and bruises litter her flesh like a mirage of her will to survive.

She wasn't going without a fight.

Fuck, she looks so broken lying there with strong, broad men moving her body around, trying to breathe life back into her. She's fading from us with each passing second. If she doesn't come back from this, none of us will.

Movement from behind them in the bathroom, snags my attention. A groaning sounds and a guy is getting to his feet inside the smashed shower stall.

"Who the fuck is that?" I snarl.

Sebastian's eyes follow mine, and he winces as he tries to stand. That's when I see the torrent of blood flowing down his back from a massive shard of glass wedged into his shoulder blade.

"He did this," he wheezes, wobbling as he manages to stand. "He fucking drowned her."

My eyes track the stranger now pulling a knife from a sheath on his belt and glaring at us. We didn't come unarmed. Both Leo and Zac had time to gather our weapons before Rick showed up and they took off with his car, but this motherfucker deserves more than a bullet. I lean down to pull my own knife from my boot. It's jagged-edged with my name carved into the steel.

He will wear my name on his insides.

Prowling past Leo, I hear the beep…beep…beep of the defib before the low hum as it shocks our girl. Her body rises and thuds against the floor.

He fucking did this to her.

He killed her.

I advance on him, and he grins, blood from his obvious tackle with Seb staining his lips.

"It was nothing personal," he hisses. "I'm just here for the paycheck. Jack has more money than sense. He didn't even notice where Marjorie was spending it. Fucking idiot. Another moron in politics."

"Oh, you're wrong," I growl. "It's way fucking personal and you've cashed your last check."

He swipes out with his knife, missing me as I dodge with ease. I bring a boot down on the side of his shin, making him nearly topple over. He gains his feet fast enough to swipe at me, missing me by an inch. He throws a punch, landing a fist to my jaw. We trade blow for blow, testing the other. The room is small and gives me plenty of surfaces to use. I grab his head and bring it down to connect with my knee, stunning him. Using his dazed status to my advantage, I ram his skull into the sink and then toilet before slashing out and cutting him across the arm with my knife.

Bleed, motherfucker.

You're going to bleed so fucking much for what you did.

He hisses in pain, grabbing his arm and spitting out the blood filling his mouth. An ugly scar pulls on his brow as he furrows them and roars before charging me. He catches me around the waist, trying to ram me backward against the sink. I slam my knife down into his back and then yank it out. He howls and throws his weight further into me, taking me to the ground. He slumps over me as he searches for the strength to keep me pinned. Straddling my waist, he attempts to force his blade down into my face, but I've weakened him too much, and I know I can overpower him.

Zac, without hesitation, approaches from behind and grabs a handful of the guy's hair. He yanks his head back and slices across his jugular at the same time I plunge my blade into his heart. Blood spurts over me, a broken tap coating me in the bastard's life source. Zac pushes the body to the ground, releasing me from beneath him.

Scrambling to my feet, both mine and Zac's eyes fall upon the unconscious Marjorie lying slumped beside the toilet. Zac checks her pulse and nods to inform me she's breathing. Picking her up, he moves through to the bedroom and dumps her on the bed.

I'm on shaky legs as I walk into the bedroom, but I weaken and collapse to my knees when I dare my gaze to Clove. Leo holds Lucky to his chest. It all comes rushing back. Harsh reality sucker punches me in the gut. Burning fire leaks from my eyes, a rock lodging in my throat. I can't do this. Not without her.

"It's okay," he tells me, maneuvering her body so I can see her beautiful face. Dark lashes flutter as her eyelids blink open. Her cheeks are still pale and thick, still-blue lips open with a delicate, soft murmur seeping from them.

"Guess I really am lucky," she croaks.

I throw myself at her, hugging both her and Leo and letting all my fear, anger, and sorrow bleed from me like an open sore. She's okay. She's fucking okay.

"I love you, Lucky," I choke out. "Damn, woman, you scared the hell outta me."

"Out of us!" Leo corrects me, his cheeks wet with tears.

"We need to get this asshole to the hospital before he bleeds out," Zac grunts, looking down at Seb, who is slouching over Lucky's legs. His blood seeps out, leaking all over her, and his face is ashen.

"And her," I say, pointing at the bed. "She might be hurt too."

"It was Marjorie," Seb groans, shifting. "She fucking stabbed me."

She what?

Zac's face flashes with fury as my mind attempts to catch up.

Marjorie?

Nerdy, librarian looking Marjorie?

"She killed my mom," Lucky sobs, gripping onto Leo's shirt. She wheezes as her eyes struggle to stay open. We need to get her seen by a fucking doctor, too.

A ragged gasp resounds from the bed and Marjorie sits bolt up like the fucking Undertaker from the WWE back in the day.

She screeches at Lucky, "You've ruined everythi—"

Pop!

Her words are silenced by the shot and she's knocked back. Marjorie's mouth hangs open as blood runs down the new hole that's in the middle of her forehead. Zac lowers his gun and hisses, "Cunt."

As we stare in stunned silence, Zac barks us into action. "Hospital. Now." He shoves his gun into his holster before scooping up Lucky from Leo's grasp and nodding for us to help Seb. "Don't make me say it again, boys. Let's go."

28

Leo King—Open Source Intelligence Agent

I've never held someone dying in my arms before. My own pulse weakened to such a degree that I truly believed if she didn't come back, my own heart would cease to beat. When she gasped for air, we *all* gasped with her. Filling our lungs and allowing ourselves to breathe.

Without Clove, there is no oxygen.

There is no life.

She's our fucking everything.

To love someone so intensely that the fate of them living determines if you even want to live yourself…it's overwhelming. And magical. Who can say they've loved that deeply? That intently?

The clatter of people moving around, coupled with the blinding, stark-white walls, gives me a headache as I sit in the waiting area with Ford and Zac. Our girl is going to be fine, but she needs to rest. Seb lost a shit-ton of blood, needed a transfusion, and thirty-eight stitches. Another war wound for the leader of our ship. If he hadn't gotten to Clove when he did, she wouldn't be here right now.

That thought makes my head thunder worse and the coffee in my stomach churn violently.

It's crazy how it can take something so dramatic to make you realize life is too fucking short and unpredictable to be living any other way than happy.

Clove is our happy.

Yes, ours.

I guess it's kind of weird. Four guys willingly sharing one woman. But she's Clove fucking Sterling. She deserves four times the usual love. Love the four of us are desperately willing to give. Our relationship might be a little unusual to the outside world, but for us, it works. It just fucking works.

"He's here," Zac grinds out, rising tiredly to his feet. My eyes travel the long corridor to see Jack marching toward us. Weary eyes seek out his daughter, but he only finds us three.

"W-Where is she? I g-got your message," he stutters, tumbling over his words.

This isn't a man who would willingly put his daughter in harm's way. This isn't a man who would approve of his daughter's attempted murder for his own political agenda. No, this is the face of a frantic father worried sick.

"First," Zac rumbles, puffing out his chest standing toe to toe with Jack. "You need to tell us if you had any idea just how far Marjorie was willing to go to get you into the White House."

Jack's security team lingers near the entrance door out of earshot. They know he'll be safe in our hands. And he will be if he has the right answers for us.

"What the hell are you talking about?" Jack demands, lines crinkling his eyes and making his lips thin into a line.

"Marjorie was behind the attempt on Clove's life," I tell him bluntly, watching him closely for a reaction.

His brows crash together in confusion at first. Then, he scowls angrily at me. "No," he scoffs, shaking his head as though the very thought is absurd. "Marjorie wouldn't hurt a damn fly and certainly wouldn't know anyone capable of hurting Clove or anyone. She's an assistant—a campaign manager."

"She tried to kill Clove, Jack," Zac growls. "Had her henchmen drown her in a motherfucking bathtub."

Ford winces at the reminder and I swallow down the bile that keeps creeping up my throat.

Jack's face falls and his hand goes to his chest as if Zac physically struck out at him. "She…is she…is my daughter…" His eyes shine with tears.

"She's fine now," I assure him. "She's going to be fine."

His body sags and his face crumples with emotion. "I think there has to be a mistake. I've known Marjorie for over a decade. She's just Marjorie." He clearly struggles to take in what we're telling him.

"Actually, she's just nothing," Zac bites out with no tact. "She's dead. I shot her in the head back at the house, so technically she's not anything."

Ford and I exchange an "oh shit" look.

Jack inhales loudly, his eyes locking with Zac's, who stares back fiercely. He's not fucking joking.

"She tried to kill Clove," Zac hisses. "Anyone who is a risk to her life will die. I don't care if it's a woman who fooled everyone for a decade or a soldier paid to do as he's told." He steps further into Jack and drops his tone so low I have to move closer to hear him when he says, "Or a father trying to further his own agenda. They fucking die."

Jack swallows loudly and nods, a smile tugging at his lips, surprising the shit out of me. Zac is a motherfucking scary ass dude.

"And I'm grateful that you take your job this seriously and that you've kept her safe," Jack says to him. "All of you. Trust me when I tell you I'd happily die for Clove if in any way I was a risk to her. But I'm not. None of this matters without her. My political career—my life, means nothing without her." His expression hardens. "Now I'm going to go see my daughter. I suggest you go to the house and get rid of any evidence of what occurred there."

"You don't want to involve the police?" I query, confused.

"Shooting people in the head is frowned upon by the law. I owe you more than I could ever repay," Jack says fiercely. "I won't allow Marjorie to ruin more lives by letting Zac get arrested for her demise."

Well, damn. We had him wrong after all.

"I'll stay," Ford assures us, following Jack down the corridor to Clove's room.

I let out a heavy sigh. I guess we're dumping bodies. I slap a hand down on Zac's shoulder and offer him a reassuring smile. "She'll be fine with Ford. Let's go sort this mess out before anyone else discovers it."

29

Clove Sterling—The Client

One week later...

You'd never know what happened in this room only a week ago. There's no trace of death, murder, chaos. I would have never thought Marjorie was capable of this whole ordeal. Now she's gone. My guys killed her for her sins against me. I feel no guilt or sorrow for her death. I don't know where they took the bodies—her and the man she used as a tool to carry out her final plan. And I don't care. All I know is they're gone. A shiver runs through me as I remember well before then. Good memories. Back when it all started with Seb, Ford, Leo, and Zac. Memories of when my world first began to change. When my guys first laid their eyes on me with new sight. I can't help but smile. But my smile falls when I think about my dad.

I chose not to tell him what Marjorie confessed about Mom. His heart is already shattered enough, little shards of guilt bleeding him out one thought at a time. He wouldn't survive knowing she was responsible for my mother as well. It would tip him over the edge. I can spare him that.

I drag the suitcase from my closet and plonk it on the bed before going to my dresser and emptying it of the contents, shoving everything inside the square box. The door peels open, and my father enters on timid feet. "Hey," he utters, grimacing when he sees me packing. "What are you doing?"

Sighing, I sit on the bed and pat the mattress for him to join me. "You can't keep me locked in your high tower forever, Dad." I nudge him, smiling. Ever since he was allowed to bring me home, he's been overbearing and anal about every security detail possible.

"I don't want to send you away," he tells me, gripping my hand and squeezing. "I'll never send you anywhere again. You belong here with me. I won't run for president. We'll spend more time together."

"I don't want you to stop being who you are," I tell him gently. "You were always destined to end up in DC, but that's your life. Not mine. I don't belong here."

"Where do you belong if not here with your father?" he asks, chuckling, but it's not amusement, it's confusion.

"I belong with them, Dad. I always have. Since the day you shut the car door on us at Mom's funeral. It's always been them. They are my life, my future, my destiny."

His brows furl together. "Clove…" He chokes a little and clears his throat, a flurry of questions dancing in his eyes as his cheeks turn ruddy with embarrassment. He doesn't need to know all the details to the thoughts racing in his mind.

"I love them," is all I say before getting to my feet and clasping the suitcase closed. "But I love you too and always will. Good luck with your campaign, Daddy." I drop a kiss to his cheek and type out a quick text.

Me: I'm ready.

Seconds later, Ford knocks and enters my room, offering me his warm, infectious smile.

"I'll take this, Lucky," he says, grabbing the suitcase and taking my hand. "Jack." He nods before gently guiding me out of the room and down the stairs to the waiting Tahoe where Zac sits, the engine idling. Seb watches me like a hawk from the passenger seat. Zac winks at me as I jump in the back, scooting over to Leo. After Ford tosses my suitcase in the back, he too slides in beside me.

"Got everything you need?" Zac asks, his eyes meeting mine in the rearview mirror.

Sebastian turns to give me a happy smile. Leo gives my thigh a squeeze. And Ford steals a kiss on my cheek.

"Yes," I tell him, overcome with happiness. "All I'll ever need is right here."

"Let's go home, then," Seb orders.

Home.

Butterflies dance in my stomach and my heart clenches in my chest.

They're *my* home.

Sebastian, Ford, Leo, and Zac.

God, I love them.

Mine.

EPILOGUE

Sebastian Constantine—Chief Protection Specialist

Six months later…

I swipe the sweat from my brow, hating that it's hot as fuck today, but thrilled as hell with the progress the builders have made. Slab has been poured and framing is up. I hired a local builder—another *friend* of Rachel's—and he's proven to be worth his weight in gold. My house no longer fits, not to mention it was mine.

This new house is ours.

Every single one of us has contributed to what we wanted out of this place. The guys wanted functional shit, but it was Clo who wanted to pick out furniture and décor. Every day she's online picking out new stuff we have to house in storage until the house is built. But at least she's happy. That's all any of us have ever hoped for.

A car pulls up the gravel drive on the new land the four of us purchased for our girl and our new home. I recognize it as Rick's. He climbs out with Rachel and Seth in tow. Seth runs over to the framed house to run around, checking out shit like kids do.

"Can't believe you're selling your property," Rachel says grumpily. "You kicked us out."

Rick rolls his eyes at me, but he's clearly amused.

"I didn't kick you out," I say with a chuckle. "I'm selling *my* property that *you* freeloaded on. Besides, I didn't leave you hanging. You're out of that trailer that scares the hell out of you every time a storm comes through."

She smirks because she knows it's true. Another buddy of mine has a ranch with horses and other livestock. He's always traveling for rodeo shows, but needs someone to keep up the property while he's gone. Since Rachel did a good job all these years with mine, I recommended her to him. Instead of staying in a dinky trailer, she gets to live in a big-ass house with a nice view.

"At least Henry pays me," she agrees. "And he doesn't mind if Rick stays over."

Rachel has always been a sleepover girl. Fast and onto the next guy. Rick sleeps over but doesn't leave. And now that she looks like she's carrying a basketball in her stomach, I don't think he'll be keen on leaving his daughter either. Eventually he'll work on her enough that she'll marry him. Zac and I are especially thankful for Rick. Now she leaves us the fuck alone.

"Did you just come to torture me?" I ask, my brows lifting in question.

She laughs, her blond ponytail swaying with the movement. "No, asshole. I came to invite you and your harem to dinner. Rick has brisket going and I made some of my famous potato salad."

Clo fucking loves her potato salad.

"Yeah, yeah, we'll be there," I grumble. "What time?"

She smirks, knowing she won the battle. Her potato salad always wins. And once Clo gave us the scare of a lifetime, Rachel held up a white flag of defeat. It was slow at first, but being that neither woman has any girlfriends, they forged a friendship that has strengthened over the past several months.

"Seven. Tell Clove to bring something chocolate. I will die unless I get chocolate. Tell her those exact words," Rachel says dramatically.

I laugh. "Got it. Chocolate and my harem. Anything else, your royal pain in the ass?"

"Nope," she says with a smile and then yells at Seth. "Let's go, baby!"

Seth gives me a hug before they all climb back into their car. I slide into my new Ford F150 extended cab truck and head home. It won't be home for long. Soon, this bigger house will be built and we'll make plenty of new memories here.

It's a twenty-minute drive back to the house, so I call Zac. He's up at the office in town. We love fucking Clo like it's our job, but the reality is we can't do that for a living. Not to mention, we'd go stir crazy and it'd only give Zac more time to think up kinky ways to truss up our girl. Not that I mind seeing her tied up and at our mercy, but we still have to put food on the table.

"Yo," he answers. "How's the house looking?"

"Awesome. They framed it fast. If we have a dry summer, we might have it finished early fall," I tell him. "How's the Briggs file?"

He launches into our newest client. Once we decided we weren't going anywhere else, we set up headquarters for Integral Defense Security in a brick building on Main Street right next to the police station. So far, we've gained jobs from aiding the police to investigating cheating husbands. Fontaine Briggs is an old man in his seventies who thinks people are poaching on his land. The man is fucking senile as all hell and is pretty sure the game wardens and forest rangers are in on the gig. But crazy or not, his dollar spends like the rest of them.

"You know, the old coot isn't as half off his rocker as everyone would like to think," Zac says with a chuckle. "All it took was a little surveillance on his property to know something's going on. One of the game wardens, Abe Frye, is a shifty-eyed fucker. I'm looking into him now. His truck sure visits Briggs' woods an awful lot and he always leaves with something tarped in the bed."

I pull into the driveway next to the Tahoe that Ford has commandeered and next to Leo's red Camaro, a car I'm pretty sure Clove sucked his dick to convince him to buy.

"I'm at the house. Gonna get cleaned up and then we have to go to Rachel's for dinner."

He groans. "Is she going to show us all her baby shit again?"

"Clove probably bought her more baby shit, so I'm going to go with yes."

"Is she making potato salad?" he asks.

"Let's be real, man, it's the only way she'll get us over there willingly."

He snorts. "See you in ten."

We hang up and I head inside the house. It's unusually quiet. I prowl through the rooms until I make it to the master. Those dirty bastards are all three naked, lying on their sides, and moaning. Leaning my shoulder on the doorframe, I watch them. Ford and Leo love double dipping in our girl. Personally, I think those two get the most joy out of rubbing their dicks together. And right now, both their dicks slide against one another as they fuck

Clo's pussy. Leo is pressed against her from behind, his face buried in her hair, while Ford is at her front. Leo and Ford work in tandem, their hips bucking in unison, as they double fuck her into oblivion. Ford's shoulder flexes as he rubs at her clit. Just watching has me hard as fuck.

But I'm sweaty and tired and don't feel like sharing.

So, I watch.

As soon as they come and the sounds coming from her body are juicy as hell, I start stripping out of my clothes. I walk through to the bathroom and turn on the shower before returning to collect my girl. Ford eases out of her and then she slides off Leo's cock. When she sees me, her face lights up with a beautiful smile.

"I missed you," she breathes, her honey eyes roaming down my chest to my erection.

"Seems like you were distracted plenty," I tease.

She bites on her bottom lip, giving me a pouty expression. "You know it takes all four of you to satisfy me fully."

My dick jolts at the reminder. "Well, I can't keep you waiting and in need." I offer her my hand, which she happily takes. Both Leo and Ford lie back on the bed, panting and exhausted from their love fest of three. I pull Clo into the bathroom where we can enjoy our party of two. She steps under the spray of the shower, the water slicking back her dark brown hair nearly to her ass. I take a moment to admire her ass. It's bigger and rounder. I fucking love it.

She must catch me staring because she turns, giving me more opportunity to adore her body. Her tits are huge these days, which none of us can seem to get enough of, but it's her cute little stomach that gets my dick hard. Pregnant with our baby. We don't know the sex yet, but will soon. I can't wait to see what the baby looks like. The alpha in me hopes it comes out with icy blue eyes and black hair like me. But I know I'll be just as happy if it comes out with green godlike eyes like Leo or a fucking smirk like Ford. Even if it comes out grumpy as fuck like Zac, we'll still love this baby. Mostly, I just want it to look like Clo. The very thought of her giving us many children to fill up our new house has me eager to make love to her.

"You're so intense today," she says, holding her arms open so I'll step into them.

I wrap her in a tight embrace, pulling her to my chest. "Just wondering how the fuck we got so lucky to have you."

She tilts her head up and gives me a sweet smile. "I'm the lucky one."

Grabbing her ass, I lift her. She eases her thighs around my waist as I slip into her tight warmth. Our mouths meet in a heated kiss as I fuck her no doubt sore pussy as gently as I can. When she digs her heels into my ass, I know the time for softness is over. My girl likes to get dirty and rough.

"Seb," she moans. "Harder. Fuck me harder, *Daddy*."

God, I fucking love her.

I chuckle against her mouth. Now that she's pregnant, she's taken to using that name a lot with all four of us. And for all the assholes who said that shit was creepy, they didn't have that name tumbling from Clo's juicy pink lips. That word sets every damn one of us off, thrumming with feral, manly pride. I kiss her hard and fuck her harder. Her head bangs against the tile, but she's not worried. As soon as she cries out in pleasure, I detonate. I fill her cunt up with my release, nipping at her lips as I do.

I've barely slid her back to her feet before Zac joins us in the shower. He strokes his dick as he gives Clo a wicked look.

"You still don't look satisfied, brat," he says, his eyes darkening with lust. "Why don't you get on your knees and I'll give you something to fill you up."

I swat her ass with a loud pop that makes her shriek before setting to soaping my body down. Clo falls to her knees, eagerly ready to suck on Zac. He threads his fingers behind his head and looks down at her. His oblique muscles flex and his hips thrust as she slides him into her mouth. My dick begins to harden again. I love watching her gag on his monstrous cock. That shit turns me the fuck on.

Movement catches my eye just outside the shower door beyond the glass. Both Leo and Ford are also stroking their dicks, hungry for another taste of our girl. We're insatiable. She turns us into starved men. Thank fuck she has enough of her to feed all four of us.

Ford opens the door and joins us, followed by Leo. One of the items on our list was a much bigger shower. For now, the four of us squish in, eagerly watching our own little porn show up close and personal.

We should shower quickly and get ready for dinner.

Or we could spend all night devouring our girl instead…

Looks like dinner is canceled.

Dessert is looking mighty fucking delicious.

The End

(If you enjoyed Share Me by Ker Dukey and K Webster, you should check out Pretty Stolen Dolls *by this dynamic duo!)*

Up Next!

I had a plan.
Make Ren Hayes pay.
But plans don't always turn out the way we want them to.

He was found not guilty of murdering my best friend.
But that doesn't make him innocent.
In my eyes, he's guilty.

Guilty of charming everyone around him into believing his innocence.
Guilty of being so intoxicating I forget who he is—what he is.
And guilty of awakening parts of me I never knew existed before his touch.

I know eventually, I'll succumb.
His allure beckons me.
Keeping me on the edge of madness between lust and hate.

In the end, it's me who's guilty.
Guilty of allowing him to take my breath away.

BOOKS BY
KER DUKEY and K WEBSTER

Pretty Little Dolls Series:

Pretty Stolen Dolls

Pretty Lost Dolls

Pretty New Doll

Pretty Broken Dolls

The V Games Series:

Vlad

Ven

Vas

KKinky Reads Collection:

Share Me

Choke Me

The Elite Seven Series:

Lust by Ker Dukey

Pride by J.D. Hollyfield

Wrath by Claire C. Riley

Envy by MN Forgy

Gluttony by K Webster

Sloth by Giana Darling

Greed by Ker Dukey and K Webster

Four Fathers Series:

Blackstone by J.D. Hollyfield

Kingston by Dani Rene

Pearson by K Webster

Wheeler by Ker Dukey

Four Sons Series:

Nixon by Ker Dukey

Hayden by J.D. Hollfield

Brock by Dani Rene

Camden by K Webster

PLAYLIST

"Back to You" by Louis Tomlinson and Bebe Rexha

"I Don't Wanna Live Forever" by Zayn

"Pillowtalk" by Zayn

"Loud(y)" by Lewis Del Mar

"The Death of Me" by Meg Myers

"War of Hearts" by Ruelle

"Love is Mystical" by Cold War Kids

"White Noise" by Badflower

"Little One" by Highly Suspect

"Where is My Mind?" by Pixies

"Blossom" by Candlebox

"#1 Crush" by Garbage

"So Real" by Jeff Buckley

"Hold Me Down" by Halsey

"Like Lovers Do" by Hey Violet

"Movement" by Hozier

"R U Mine?" by Arctic Monkeys

"Sex on Fire" by Kings of Leon

"Like Real People Do" by Hozier

"Wild Horses" by Bishop Briggs

"Can I Exist" by MISSIO

"Tempt My Trouble" by Bishop Briggs

"I Feel Love" by Donna Summer

"Sweet Young Thing Ain't Sweeet No More" by Mudhoney

ACKNOWLEDGMENTS

KER DUKEY

This exciting project was one we planned for a long time, and we kept putting it down to complete other things. I'm so happy we took our time and finally got around to *sharing* it with our amazing readers.

It's always a pleasure writing with Kristi. We have so much fun creating worlds and characters together, but this one was extra fun! Share Me is one in a long line of sexy reads we have planned and I haven't had this much fun writing in a long time. It's refreshing and fun, sexy and alluring. Kristi, thank you for always agreeing to leap with me. You're not just my co-writer, you're my true friend who I lean on and admire. You're the one to picks me up and shakes me when I need it and remind me we're badass and can do anything. You're the one I want to share with when a new idea comes to me at the most stupid of times. And you are the one who I want to create new worlds with. Let's take over this bitch! Love you a 1000%!

To Dukey's darKER souls & Krazy for Webster's groups, thank you for your love, enthusiasm, and help to get the word out about these titles. You are the real rockstars. We adore you.

To our readers. There are never the right words to describe how thankful I am that you pick up a title of mine/ ours. To explore worlds with me/us and keep my/our characters in your mind and heart is a gift to us. Thank you! I/we hope never to let you down. To keep bringing you new, exciting stories and characters that you want to explore and keep. Readers are explorers, dreamers, inventors. Keep living a million lives within the pages.

To the people who make it happen:

Emily A. Lawrence, our editor for this book, thank you for being professional and for making our little world perfect.

Beta readers, thank you so much for your feedback. You girls never fail us. We love you dearly.

Stacey, our formatter, as always no one does it like you, woman. Thanks for always making our books BEAUTIFUL.

Cover designer, Amy Queue, THANK YOU! I know we were fussy haha, but you did amazing with no complaints. We adore this cover. Thank you.

Bloggers, thanks so much for taking a chance on our new title. For all your support and effort in getting our work in the hands of the readers. Thank you for taking the time to read and review for us. We appreciate you.

PR & PA's—Terrie & Misty, you guys, keep us running, thank you for all you do.

Nicole, thank you for all your work getting our media packages out there. You rock.

ACKNOWLEDGMENTS

K WEBSTER

Thank you to my husband…I love that you support me even when I say I'm going to write a book about one heroine and four heroes. You "get" me in a way no one else can.

A 1000% thank you to Ker Dukey for being such an awesome friend and co-writer! We have such a blast coming up with these stories and then executing them! I think part of our fun is our banter and video chats! You're a true friend and I love you to the moon and back. You're the Dr. Dre to my Eminem, and collaborating in the lab with you is where we make magic happen. Love you, Ker Bear!! Can't wait to make more book babies with you!

A huge thank you to my Krazy for K Webster's Books reader group. You all are insanely supportive and I can't thank you enough.

A gigantic thank you to those who always help me out. Elizabeth Clinton, Ella Stewart, Misty Walker, Holly Sparks, Jillian Ruize, Gina Behrends, Rosa Saucedo, J.D. Hollyfield, and Nikki Ash—you ladies are my rock!

Great thanks to Ker's betas for helping make sure this book as awesome as can be! Couldn't have done it without you: PA Allison and Teresa Nicholson. Your final eyes were so helpful!

Thank you so much to Misty for always supporting my unusual journeys. I know that you're always first in line to read and cheer me on. I love you, lady!

A big thank you to my author friends who have given me your friendship and your support. You have no idea how much that means to me.

Thank you to all of my blogger friends both big and small that go above and beyond to always share my stuff. You all rock! #AllBlogsMatter

Emily A. Lawrence, thank you SO much for editing this book. You rock!!

Thank you Stacey Blake for being amazing as always when formatting my books and in general. I love you! I love you! I love you!

A big thanks to my PR gal, Nicole Blanchard. You are fabulous at what you do and keep me on track!

Lastly but certainly not least of all, thank you to all of the wonderful readers out there who are willing to hear my story and enjoy my characters like I do. It means the world to me!

ABOUT KER DUKEY

My books all tend to be darker romance, the edge of your seat, angst-filled reads. My advice to my readers when starting one of my titles… prepare for the unexpected.

I have always had a passion for storytelling, whether it be through lyrics or bedtime stories with my sisters growing up.

My mom would always have a book in her hand when I was young and passed on her love for reading, inspiring me to venture into writing my own. Not all love stories are made from light- some are created in darkness but are just as powerful and worth telling.

When I'm not lost in the world of characters, I love spending time with my family. I'm a mom and that comes first in my life, but when I do get down time, I love attending music concerts or reading events with my younger sister.

News Letter sign up: eepurl.com/OpJxT
Website: authorkerdukey.com
Facebook: www.facebook.com/KerDukeyauthor
Twitter: twitter.com/KerDukeyauthor
Instagram: www.instagram.com/kerdukey
BookBub: www.bookbub.com/profile/ker-dukey
Goodreads: www.goodreads.com/author/show/7313508.Ker_Dukey

Contact me here:
Ker: Kerryduke34@gmail.com
Ker's PA: terriesin@gmail.com

ABOUT
K WEBSTER

K Webster is the *USA Today* bestselling author of over seventy-five romance books in many different genres including contemporary romance, historical romance, paranormal romance, dark romance, sci-fi romance, romantic suspense, taboo romance, and erotic romance. When not spending time with her hilarious and handsome husband and two adorable children, she's active on social media connecting with her readers.

Her other passions besides writing include reading and graphic design. K can always be found in front of her computer chasing her next idea and taking action. She looks forward to the day when she will see one of her titles on the big screen.

oin K Webster's newsletter to receive a couple of updates a month on new releases and exclusive content. To join, all you need to do is go here (www.authorkwebster.com).

Facebook:www.facebook.com/authorkwebster
Blog:authorkwebster.wordpress.com
Twitter:twitter.com/KristiWebster
Email:kristi@authorkwebster.com
Goodreads:www.goodreads.com/user/show/10439773-k-webster
Instagram:instagram.com/kristiwebster

BOOKS BY
KER DUKEY

Empathy Series:

Empathy

Desolate

Vacant—Novella

Deadly—Novella

The Broken Series:

The Broken

The Broken Parts of Us

The Broken Tethers That Bind Us—Novella

The Broken Forever—Novella

The Men by Numbers Series:

Ten

Six

Drawn to You Duet:

Drawn to You

Lines Drawn

Standalone Novels:

My Soul Keeper

Lost

I See You

The Beats in Rift

Devil

Co-Written with D. Sidebottom

The Deception Series:

FaCade

Cadence

Beneath Innocence—Novella

The Lilith's Army MC Series:

Taking Avery

Finding Rhiannon

Coming Home TBA

Co-Written with K Webster

The Pretty Little Dolls Series:

Pretty Stolen Dolls

Pretty Lost Dolls

Pretty New Doll

Pretty Broken Dolls

The V Games Series:

Vlad

Ven

Vas

KKinky Reads Collection:

Share Me

Choke Me

Joint Series

Four Fathers Series:

Blackstone by J.D. Hollyfield

Kingston by Dani René

Pearson by K Webster

Wheeler by Ker Dukey

Four Sons Series:

Nixon by Ker Dukey

Hayden by J.D Hollyfield

Brock by Dani René

Camden by K Webster

The Elite Seven Series:

Lust—Ker Dukey

Pride—J.D. Hollyfield

Wrath—Claire C. Riley

Envy—M.N.Forgy

Gluttony—K Webster

Sloth—Giana Darling

Greed—Ker Dukey & K Webster

BOOKS BY K WEBSTER

Psychological Romance Standalones:

My Torin

Whispers and the Roars

Cold Cole Heart

Blue Hill Blood

Romantic Suspense Standalones:

Dirty Ugly Toy

El Malo

Notice

Sweet Jayne

The Road Back to Us

Surviving Harley

Love and Law

Moth to a Flame

Erased

Extremely Forbidden Romance Standalones:

The Wild

Hale

Like Dragonflies

Taboo Treats:

Bad Bad Bad

Coach Long

Ex-Rated Attraction

Mr. Blakely

Easton

Crybaby

Lawn Boys

Malfeasance

Renner's Rules

The Glue

Dane

Enzo

Red Hot Winter

KKinky Reads Collection:

Share Me

Choke Me

Contemporary Romance Standalones:

The Day She Cried

Untimely You

Heath

Sundays are for Hangovers

A Merry Christmas with Judy

Zeke's Eden

Schooled by a Senior

Give Me Yesterday

Sunshine and the Stalker

Bidding for Keeps

B-Sides and Rarities

Paranormal Romance Standalones:

Apartment 2B

Running Free

Mad Sea

War & Peace Series:

This is War, Baby (Book 1)

This is Love, Baby (Book 2)

This Isn't Over, Baby (Book 3)

This Isn't You, Baby (Book 4)

This is Me, Baby (Book 5)

This Isn't Fair, Baby (Book 6)

This is the End, Baby (Book 7—a novella)

Lost Planet Series:

The Forgotten Commander (Book 1)

The Vanished Specialist (Book 2)

2 Lovers Series:

Text 2 Lovers (Book 1)

Hate 2 Lovers (Book 2)

Thieves 2 Lovers (Book 3)

Pretty Little Dolls Series:

Pretty Stolen Dolls (Book 1)

Pretty Lost Dolls (Book 2)

Pretty New Doll (Book 3)

Pretty Broken Dolls (Book 4)

The V Games Series:

Vlad (Book 1)

Ven (Book 2)

Vas (Book 3)

Four Fathers Books:

Pearson

Four Sons Books:

Camden

Elite Seven Books:

Gluttony

Not Safe for Amazon Books:

The Wild

Hale

Bad Bad Bad

This is War, Baby

Like Dragonflies

The Breaking the Rules Series:

Broken (Book 1)

Wrong (Book 2)

Scarred (Book 3)

Mistake (Book 4)

Crushed (Book 5—a novella)

The Vegas Aces Series:

Rock Country (Book 1)

Rock Heart (Book 2)

Rock Bottom (Book 3)

The Becoming Her Series:

Becoming Lady Thomas (Book 1)

Becoming Countess Dumont (Book 2)

Becoming Mrs. Benedict (Book 3)

Alpha & Omega Duet:

Alpha & Omega (Book 1)

Omega & Love (Book 2)

Printed in Great Britain
by Amazon